Twelve hot heroes.
One burning question.

Don't miss a story in Harlequin Blaze's
12-book continuity series, featuring irresistible
soldiers from all branches of the armed forces.

Heat up your holidays with A Few Good Marines...

DEVIL IN DRESS BLUES
by Karen Foley
October 2011

MODEL MARINE
by Candace Havens
November 2011

RED-HOT SANTA
by Tori Carrington
December 2011

Uniformly Hot!—
The Few. The Proud. The Sexy as Hell!

Available wherever Harlequin books are sold.

Dear Reader,

What do *you* want for Christmas? Dangerous
question, depending on who you ask. Of course, if
a *Red-Hot Santa* is involved, I'm thinking many of us
might make a nice, long list, if only so we could sit
on his lap: again...and again...and again....

In our latest Uniformly Hot! book, Jackson Savage
(younger brother of Jason from *Undeniable Pleasures*)
is the epitome of all things steamy...something his
longtime best friend Maxine McGuire has always
known, but never allowed herself to sample. Until
now. But does the mind-blowing chemistry they share
between the sheets translate into love? Or is it just
GREAT sex?

I hope Jackson and Max's sexy journey heats up those
cold winter nights and that you enjoy this latest
Lazarus Security title. We'd love to hear what you
think. Contact us at P.O. Box 12271, Toledo, OH 43612,
or visit us on the web at www.toricarrington.net or
www.facebook.com/toricarrington.

Happy holidays!

Lori & Tony Karayianni
a.k.a. Tori Carrington

Tori Carrington

RED-HOT SANTA

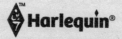

TORONTO NEW YORK LONDON
AMSTERDAM PARIS SYDNEY HAMBURG
STOCKHOLM ATHENS TOKYO MILAN MADRID
PRAGUE WARSAW BUDAPEST AUCKLAND

Recycling programs
for this product may
not exist in your area.

ISBN-13: 978-0-373-79656-4

RED-HOT SANTA

Copyright © 2011 by Lori Karayianni & Tony Karayianni

This edition published by arrangement with Harlequin Books S.A.

For questions and comments about the quality of this book
please contact us at Customer_eCare@Harlequin.ca.

® and TM are trademarks of the publisher. Trademarks indicated with
® are registered in the United States Patent and Trademark Office, the
Canadian Trade Marks Office and in other countries.

www.Harlequin.com

Printed in U.S.A.

ABOUT THE AUTHOR

RT Book Reviews Career Achievement Award-winning bestselling duo Lori Schlachter Karayianni and Tony Karayianni are the power behind the pen name Tori Carrington. Their more than fifty novels include numerous Harlequin Blaze miniseries, as well as the ongoing Sofie Metropolis comedic mystery series with another publisher. Visit www.toricarrington.net and www.sofiemetro.com for more information on the couple and their titles.

Books by Tori Carrington

To get the inside scoop on Harlequin Blaze and its talented writers, be sure to check out blazeauthors.com.

All backlist available in ebook.

We dedicate this book to servicemen and women in all military branches everywhere for not only putting their lives on the line on a daily basis, but for the heartache they must endure when serving so far away from the ones they love. And to editor extraordinaire Brenda Chin...just because....

_1_

HIS BROTHER WAS a dumbass. It was as simple and as complicated as that.

Jackson Savage tugged on the suspenders holding up the too-big red velvet pants he had on over his jeans. He'd stripped out of the red jacket some time ago, leaving him frustrated at being the one who got stuck wearing the Santa suit for the bar's Christmas party. The hat and shiny black boots remained intact even though he'd prefer to ditch them, as well. But he was scheduled to play Santa later so he thought he'd better keep them on.

Thank God this was his last night working at the bar. Even if his brother wouldn't be happy about it.

Oh, he knew there were valid reasons his older sibling felt protective of him. Losing their parents at a young age was the biggest of them. Thinking he needed to be a father figure as a result was another. But as far as Jackson was concerned, he'd grown beyond the nose-blowing stage long ago. It was past time Jason took a good look at him and realized he wasn't a kid anymore.

If his brother didn't…well, he was afraid he was going to have to kick his ass just to prove his point. And that would be one fight neither of them would walk away from unscathed, he was sure.

Well, that was adult of him, wasn't it? Jackson grimaced at the asinine thought and swiped the white puff of the Santa hat back from his brow.

Still, nearly four months had passed since he'd proven himself up for the job, not only as a responsible adult and decorated Marine, but solid Lazarus Security material. If taking a bullet for the cause wasn't enough, what was?

Jackson shoved the glass of draught beer he'd just filled from a tap a little too forcefully, spilling a good inch of it as he served his countless drink at The Barracks that night. He muttered an apology and then wiped the spot, topping off the glass before presenting it to one of the regulars again.

"Hey, Jax, that's the third time tonight. What's the matter?" Winston asked. "Trouble with Mrs. Claus?"

Pete, the guy standing next to him, laughed. "There'd have to be a Mrs. Claus in order for there to be trouble with her. No, Jax here's trouble is that he needs a little…something from a Mrs. Claus candidate."

Jackson gave a perfunctory laugh. "What I need

is a nice, long vacation. Preferably somewhere warm. Where someone else serves me."

Genie, one of the three waitresses, stepped up to the bar in her Santa hat, too-tight white tank and red velvet shorts trimmed in white fur, The Barracks' holiday uniform even if it was December and ten below outside. "I'll wait on you," she offered with her trademark purr.

Pete gave a low whistle. "Son, if I were you, I'd be all over that."

"Against bar policy," Jackson said absently.

Even if it wasn't, it was against *his* personal policy. He made it a point not to sleep with coworkers. He'd seen his fair share of bad episodes when things went south—as they inevitably did. South? On one unforgettable occasion, he'd ended up with a psycho bitch from hell stalking him because he'd given in to temptation and slept with her one night. It was all he'd been in the market for at the time. Apparently, she'd had other ideas. And when sweet persuasion hadn't worked, she'd resorted to other more disturbing measures to prove her love for him.

No way was he going that route again.

No matter how difficult his hot coworkers sometimes made it for him. He looked over Genie's generous curves and then up at her suggestive smile. She made his four-month-old wound itch.

But that's not why he was there. His tending bar was really only a way to keep himself occupied until his brother came around. Yeah, it helped pay the bills, but considering the large, structured settlement and trust fund he and Jason had received upon their parents' deaths, he didn't need the money.

Still, he'd barely touched his bank account, gaining a certain satisfaction in supporting himself and his day-to-day expenses with his income. Right now, his life resembled some sort of airplane holding pattern. He only hoped he'd be cleared for landing soon, because he didn't know how much fuel he had left before he crashed.

He checked his cell phone, knowing as he did who he was hoping he'd find a call or text from. And, strangely enough, it wasn't his brother. He'd smiled when Max McGuire's missed call had popped up in this display. She hadn't left a message, but that was no surprise; she never did.

Max...

His movements slowed as he realized he missed her.

It had been a while since they'd spoken. The last time he'd talked to her, she'd been somewhere out in the Pacific Northwest working for some sort of high-end security firm. Their longtime friendship had always gone through ebbs and flows, with stretches where an occasional phone call was the name of the game.

Then there were the times when they'd been

"thick as thieves," as Gram liked to say, nearly inseparable.

Of course, the physical distance between them currently prevented that.

Still, over the years they made sure to carve out some together time, meeting for at least a few days to catch up, usually on some sort of physical adventure, like mountain climbing or wild water kayaking.

He thought he should call her back, maybe see about scheduling just such a trip soon. Or perhaps he'd go visit her, see what she was up to and how life was treating her.

Jackson told his boss, Chuck, that he was taking his break. He grabbed his leather jacket and let himself out from behind the bar. He returned a few greetings as he walked to the back and then through the door leading to the alley behind the row of buildings. He leaned against the cold brick and shoved his hands deep into his jacket pockets. Closing his eyes, he took a deep breath. It was at times like these he wished he still smoked.

"Hey," a female said next to him.

He hadn't realized anyone else was out here. "Hey," he said without opening his eyes.

"Cold out, huh?"

If he hadn't been able to tell by her deep inhale, the acrid scent of cigarette smoke would have revealed what she was doing.

"That it is," he said.

"You work here?"

"Yeah."

"This is my first time at this bar." He heard her shoes shuffle in the salt they put down as a de-icer. "My friends suggested it. I haven't been inside yet…"

Her voice sounded familiar.

He cracked his eyelids open and openly regarded the pretty redhead.

Holy shit.

"Max? Is that you?"

FOR A MOMENT Maxine McGuire was afraid Jackson wouldn't recognize her. And that was beyond stupid, really. He was her best friend. They'd pretty well grown up together on the farm as kids, and had been together again for a brief stint when they'd been stationed overseas in the Marines. But it had been a good two years since their physical paths last crossed, despite their sometimes lengthy telephone conversations. And while she wasn't about to tell him, a big part of the reason she'd chosen The Barracks as the place to meet her old high school friends, instead of the countless other bars in the military hub of Colorado Springs, Colorado, was because Jackson tended there.

For reasons she couldn't fathom, she always experienced a spark of fear he wouldn't recognize her. That too much time had passed, or maybe he was otherwise occupied…

Liar.

She knew why she felt that way. Or she had an idea anyway.

While they'd always been close friends, she realized she'd always been more than a little bit in love with him. And the worst thing that could ever happen would be that he wouldn't recognize her. Or that she'd look at him and see indifference in his eyes.

Not that she ever had.

Still, she was pathetic. And it was that very self-esteem issue she hoped to finally nip totally in the bud.

Her relationship with Jax was the only area in her life she experienced such vulnerable emotions. Otherwise she was confident, strong and knew exactly where she was at any given moment and where she was going.

"Hey, Jax," she said, hoping the smile that warmed her to her toes wasn't too obvious.

He stared at her for a full minute and then pushed from the building. She stiffened as he gave her a hug. It was silly, really, because he'd always given her the same, brotherly greeting.

The problem was that her reaction had never been quite the sisterly one he was going for.

Not that he ever appeared to have a clue.

Of course, she knew she was the primary reason for that. She'd never let him in on her true feelings.

"I was just thinking about you," he said. "You called the other day but didn't leave a message."

"I never leave a message."

His chuckle tickled her ear. "Yeah, I know."

He stepped back and looked her over, as if seeing her for the first time. It was all she could do to maintain his gaze, and not to pat down her too curly hair.

"You look good," he said.

"Thanks. So do you."

She took another hit off the cigarette—her first in almost two years—and then flicked it to the ground farther down the alley.

How old had she been when they first met? Five? Six? She and her mom had just moved in with her aunt after her parents' breakup and she'd run away. It was the first of many doomed attempts, complete with a stick to ward off unwanted critters, the end tied with a handkerchief that held a sandwich, her favorite paperback novel and a pack of matches.

It had probably taken her a whole half hour to reach the Savage barn on the neighboring property, but everything was relative and she could have sworn it had been five hours and that she'd reached the border of New Mexico, at least.

She'd just spread out her handkerchief on the fresh straw, sat on it and opened her sandwich when a shadow fell across the open doorway. There stood Jackson Savage, no older than her, arms crossed over his chest. He'd told her in no uncertain terms she was on private property and that meant she was trespassing.

So she'd gathered up her things and began to stalk from the barn. He'd caught her by the arms and told her he was just kidding…then introduced himself.

She'd wasted no time tackling him to the ground and punching him. Then she'd grabbed her stick and continued on her way.

And so began their lifelong friendship, as he liked to say whenever he told the story, usually adding a bloody nose to the equation. Namely, his.

For her, well…she'd fallen in love on the spot. And she'd always found some sort of asinine way to cover up the unwanted emotion…until now.

Now she was determined to let him know exactly what she had in mind…and exactly how she felt. But she'd take it slow, hoping it would guarantee something enduring…and not send him running flat out in the opposite direction.

The reason for her change of mind? She'd come to realize there was no going forward in any of her relationships until she went back.

"I'd better get inside," she said, giving him her best smile.

She slowly slid a piece of gum into her mouth and then offered him a piece. He appeared so distracted by her movements, he didn't even see the gum.

"What? Oh. Yeah. Me, too."

She was self-conscious as she led the way back

inside, forcing herself not to fight him over control of the door. She slipped out of her coat as she walked with slow, measured steps, satisfied at the sound of his breath hissing through his teeth. Yeah, she looked good in the tight jeans and low-cut shirt she had on. She knew that. And she was pleased that he did, too.

"Here, I'll stash your coat behind the bar with mine," he said.

"Thanks." She handed her jacket over, put on her Santa hat and then applied lip-gloss. She slid the tube into a tiny inside pocket of her jeans. "I haven't seen some of these friends for years. How do I look?" she asked.

"Huh?" It seemed to take him a moment to register her question. "Oh. Great. Fine. You look good."

Great to fine to good. *Definitely* the wrong direction.

But that was Jax for you. Getting a compliment from him had always been like pulling teeth.

Good thing she'd recently decided he needed to make an appointment with the dentist...

Friends. Best friends. That's what they'd always been. He'd had her back, and she'd had his. When neither of them were in a relationship, they'd sought out each other for company. Platonic company. From swimming in the Keys, kayaking the Colorado River, day-long hikes through whatever remote forest they could find, she'd always enjoyed his company. Sometimes they'd talk about their struggles with understanding the opposite sex, as if they didn't qualify for the status, but most times they joked, challenged and dared each other.

Then there'd been those occasions when simple platonic affection had threatened to balloon into much more...

Merely remembering the times they'd wrestled around on the ground, or playfully tussled in the water, her sexual awareness taking her breath away, made her all hot and bothered.

Jackson...well, Jackson was as hot as they came. All golden haired goods looks and animal magnetism.

But it was much more than that. Much, much more. She knew what the man himself was made of. She knew that beating in his chest was a heart of gold that left him loyal to his family, doing anything for his grandmother and brother Jason...and loyal to his friends. She knew he'd be the first to stand in the face of danger, to put his life on the line if he knew it might save someone else's.

It was in those moments when barriers dropped, that she glimpsed what life might be like for them as a couple...

And she'd turned away, always refusing herself the indulgence. She was afraid of the enormity of her emotions, afraid of tarnishing their friendship.

And afraid of leaving herself vulnerable. While

threat of physical pain had never fazed her, leaving her heart exposed and unprotected scared the living daylights out of her.

If only because she'd witnessed firsthand what it had done to her mother.

Done to their family.

Now...

Well, now was different. She was no longer that rebellious girl who'd run away and holed up in his barn. The girl afraid of her emotions...and of him.

Now she wanted to push that envelope, dive into those depths, explore them, face her one and only fear.

She needed to learn that untouched side of her, the one she'd ignored, neglected and tried to shut out.

She needed to feel him...

HOLY SHIT.

The two words wound around Jackson's brain as he watched Max sitting with her friends. He kept looking for reasons to talk to her but there never seemed to be an opportunity, considering one non-stop flow of thirsty customers who kept him busy. And he never saw her go out back for another smoke break.

He scratched his head as he rang up the latest order, looking for her again in the smoky mirror behind the bar. She was standing in front of the old fashioned jukebox considering the selections. His gaze fell to her nicely rounded backside and then up to where the soft cotton of her top clung to breasts fuller than he remembered. His back stiffened as he watched a guy approach her. Not just any guy, but Tom, whom they referred to as the bar "manwhore." Just the type Max would hate on sight.

He braced himself, wondering if Tom would take it to the head or the gut.

Here it comes…

He watched as Tom not too nonchalantly slid his hand over her back, down toward her bottom. Max easily avoided the move and actually smiled before heading back to her table.

Jackson blinked. Who was this woman? She looked the same. Well, for the most part. The red curls were the same except they appeared smoother, somehow. Less wild. Her eyes were the same green but appeared brighter. And was she wearing makeup?

Jackson was confused. The Max he knew wouldn't be caught dead in that sexy outfit, not before or during her stint in the Marines, much less handle what she just had with smiling ease. She'd have been much more likely to twist the guy's arm behind his back and shove his face into the jukebox until he apologized for the unwanted advance.

Jackson met her gaze in the mirror and that mysterious smile she'd been offering him all night made a command appearance.

Holy shit.

Where was the easy camaraderie they always enjoyed? The knowing that came along with their life-long friendship?

Christ, he felt like a twelve-year-old kid in the throes of his first crush.

And that was not something he was used to feeling toward a woman who was essentially his best friend.

Hell, it wasn't something he was used to feeling, period.

This went well beyond physical attraction—which should be enough to cause concern when it came to Max...

His brain froze.

No way he was going where his thoughts and unfamiliar emotions were attempting to lead him. It was bad enough he recognized the desire to touch her in ways he never had before. To consider anything more would be akin to emotional suicide.

"Hey, did you get that, Savage?" Chuck asked.

He blinked at the bar owner. As en ex-Marine, Chuck Thomas had a healthy respect for military kindred and ran a tight operation. When things got busy, so did he. Of course, it didn't help that Chuck wasn't happy Jackson would no longer be working at the bar. He'd made noises about looking to sell the place, and admitted he had hoped Jackson might be interested. Jackson had been surprised, but quick to tell Chuck it wasn't in the cards for him.

"Sorry," he said to his taciturn boss now, keeping the peace. "I was working up the last order. Afraid I overcharged."

"Better than under. I asked for two pitchers of light and six glasses. Can you handle it?"

"Got it."

Jackson took a deep breath, telling himself he really needed to get a grip. This was Max, for Pete's sake. It wasn't like he didn't know her. And Lord knew he'd never reacted this way toward her before. She was like a sister to him, for crying out loud.

He cleared his throat. Oh, yeah? If she was like a sister, then certain body parts told him what he was contemplating was very, very wrong, indeed.

"Hey, Jax."

Her greeting nearly caused him to spill the pitcher he'd just filled. He put it on a tray along with the other one.

"Hey," he said.

He finished the order and Genie picked up the tray. He didn't miss the long look she gave Max.

"I've been meaning to ask, when did you get back into town?" he asked. It couldn't have been long. He'd have heard something before now. Then he remembered her phone call. "The last I knew, you were kicking around Oregon."

"Washington."

He smiled. "Close enough."

"Yeah." She pushed up her sleeves, drawing his

attention to the too-tight top and the full breasts underneath. Had she always had those? Why hadn't he noticed before? "I got back late last week."

"Staying long?"

She tilted her head. "Don't know yet. Depends…"

He met her gaze, seeing a question in there he didn't quite know how to interpret. Then again, he was having a hard time reading her tonight, period. Or, rather, he was finding it impossible to read his new, unfamiliar reaction to her.

"On what?"

"On whether or not I can scare up some work. You wouldn't happen to have a line on anything, would you?"

"What are you looking for?"

"Something I'm qualified for that doesn't require I learn how to use a beer tap. No offense."

He grinned. "None taken." He ignored Chuck's shout for him to get a move on. "Tonight's my last night. I start at Pegasus Security tomorrow."

"Pegasus? Is that Jason's place?"

It seemed she'd been around long enough to hear what his brother had been up to. Small towns were like that. "No. That's Lazarus."

Her full lips twisted a bit, likely seeing more than he was comfortable with just then.

He cleared his throat. "Anyway, Pegasus is actively looking for people with your job skills if you want to check them out."

"Great. Thanks."

He found himself staring at her yet again. What was up with him? He hadn't been this quiet since Jason had tried to superglue his tongue to the roof of his mouth when he was five.

"I was wondering..." she said.

He forced himself to blink up into her eyes. He wondered if she'd caught him staring again at her chest. "Wondering, um, what?"

"Can you give me a ride home later?"

It took a moment for her question to register. The fact that he was trying hard as hell not to look back at her breasts wasn't helping matters any, either. "Where?"

"My aunt's."

He dragged the back of his wrist across his brow. Was he sweating? "You're staying at your aunt's?"

She nodded. "She dropped me off, but if you're going out to your grandmother's, well, it'd be easier than asking one of the girls to run me all the way back out there."

He hadn't planned to go to Gram's tonight—there was a small apartment above the bar he rented—but the idea of spending uninterrupted time with Max so he could figure out what the hell was going on between them was too tempting to pass up.

"Sure. It'll probably be late, since I'm closing."

"That's fine. I can wait." She smiled that smile again and his jeans tightened. He adjusted the suspenders, happy for the first time that night to be wearing the blasted, baggy Santa pants. "Thanks. I appreciate it."

"No problem."

"Talk to you later, then."

"Yeah…later."

His response came after she'd already turned to walk back to her table, the view of her backside just as enticing as the view of her front.

There was chuckling down the bar. He glanced over at Winston and Pete.

"Hey, Jax," they called out. "You finally going to take care of that little problem?"

They both gave him a thumbs-up as he turned to walk down to the other end of the bar where there were other customers waiting to be served…

2

MAXINE ENJOYED CATCHING UP with her old girlfriends from high school. She might be as different as light and shadow from them, but she was pleasantly surprised they were connected in a comforting way. She'd spent so much time fraternizing with the guys in recent years—partly because she'd believed them easier to be around, mostly because as a female in the military, guys were what you tended to be around most—she'd forgotten how nice it was to have a drink with girlfriends.

Patience Saunders had been a varsity football cheerleader and an unlikely but fun friend. Her athletic ability had extended beyond short skirts and pom-poms so she and Max had participated in many of the same sports. Max wasn't surprised she was now a Phys Ed teacher at the same grammar school they'd once attended...or that she was married with two kids under two.

Julie and Jae Jennings were identical twins but had gone out of their way to disguise that fact even when their mother had tried to dress them alike as kids. When Jae had stumbled across goth fashion, she'd latched on to it tightly, and even now favored black nail polish and hinted at body piercings beyond the one visible on her left nostril.

Still, as much as Max was enjoying catching up with them, her gaze endlessly trailed to the man behind the bar, noting how'd he changed...and how her feelings had stayed the same.

"God, Jax is still as hot as he was in high school, isn't he?" Patience said with a sigh, propping her chin in her palm as she watched the man in question.

"Is he ever," Julie echoed.

Jae gave an eye roll and downed her third shot of Jaeger. "You guys always were about as subtle as a bulldozer."

"What?" Patience asked, batting her eyes in feigned innocence.

"You don't think he knows y'all are staring at him like a pack of bitches in heat?"

Julie nearly choked on the red wine she was in the middle of swallowing.

"Didn't you two used to have something?" Patience asked, turning to Max.

Max knew a moment of panic, just as she always did when someone made a similar inquiry, afraid her expression or body language had given something away. Then she realized her friends weren't being specific and relaxed. "Who? Me and Jax?" She shook her head. "Nah. We were just good friends. We still are."

Jae snorted. "Right. That's why the place nearly bursts into flames every time you two look at each other. I had to take off my jacket so I wouldn't burn up."

"What's he doing now?"

Max followed Julie's gaze to where Jax was putting on a Santa Claus coat and coming out from behind the bar. The waitress in the skimpy uniform took great pleasure in helping fix his hat.

"Looks like Santa's about to give someone what they want," Jae said drily…

CHUCK MADE THE announcement that Santa was going to take requests and have pictures taken for a $5 donation to the veterans fund. Jackson put the red jacket back on, but left it open; hell, he'd boil alive if he closed it.

Of course, Genie made him regret the decision when she sidled up to him, playing role of "helper" a little too overtly for his liking. She slid her hands inside the coat and gave him a sexy snuggle before reaching up to straighten his cap. Her flirty moves earned hoots and hollers from the guys, but all he could do was look beyond her to where Max was watching the display with an amused smile on her beautiful face.

"Hey, I wanna sit on Santa's helper's lap," Pete shouted.

"That'll cost you a hundred," Chuck told him.

They all laughed as Genie pulled up a chair next to the jukebox and pushed Jackson back to sit in it. Given her moves, he was half afraid she was going to strip off what little of her holiday outfit she wore, but instead she turned and along with the other two waitresses, went around the room collecting money from the patrons.

For the next half hour, Jackson was squashed by several of the heavier guys, slobbered on by the drunken wife of another and then sat staring at where Patience Saunders stood behind a smiling Max. He thought the night would never be over.

Then, before he could prepare himself, Max was sitting in his lap. And evidence of his instant arousal was pressed against her hot bottom...

MAX WAS UNPREPARED for Patience's none too subtle shove. She grabbed onto Jax's shoulders to keep from sliding off his lap, the hard length of his manhood through his clothing telling her things he might not have revealed in any other way.

Okay, so maybe she'd had one brew too many. But he hadn't had any. And the way he looked at her this up close and personal told her that Jae may have been a little closer to the mark than she realized: Jackson Savage wanted her.

The recognition was more intoxicating than anything this bar could offer.

Max caught herself licking her lips and stopped. She'd been here before, this mysterious place when her body betrayed her true emotions for the man beneath her. Awareness surged everywhere their bodies made contact swirling, through her bloodstream, tightening her nipples and dampening her inner thighs.

This was usually the point—where the spark of arousal promised to blaze into much more—when she would withdraw, physically and emotionally, putting much needed distance between them.

But this time...

She merely sat, holding his gaze, allowing the sizzling current to bond them in a way she never had before.

"So..." he said so quietly she nearly didn't hear him, his hands hot on her hips.

She watched his pupils dilate in his blue eyes and the way his gaze seemed drawn to her mouth.

"What do you, um, want...?"

What would happen if she told him? If she said she wanted to be sitting on his lap, with no clothes between them? To feel his hard length inside her rather than pressing against her? To see if his mouth tasted as good as it looked?

To know if the longing she'd felt for him for

so long was purely physical…or if it was much much more.

A flashbulb went off.

For a minute, Max thought it might be something of her own conjuring, but when she followed Jackson's stare to the bar bunny waitress who'd just taken their picture, she knew it wasn't.

She'd come home to Colorado to find the truth.

She'd either finally pursue her unspoken feelings for Jackson, or squash them altogether. It was time for her to move on, one way or the other.

Still, she just wasn't prepared to do that in front of God and everyone.

She also wasn't prepared for what she felt for her to burgeon even further, nearly overwhelming her, blotting out all else until a camera flash snapped her back to reality.

Had she really nearly kissed him in the middle of a bar while everyone watched?

Yes, she realized, she had.

She moved to get to her feet. Jackson helped her, standing up, as well. She noticed the way he plucked at his suit even as she smoothed her damp palms over her jeans.

"Okay, everyone, that's all for now. Santa's got work to do," he said.

And so did she, Max silently noted.

Because if he'd given away what he had in that one moment, she could only imagine what she had.

Then again, isn't that what she wanted? For him to see how she truly felt?

Yes. It was.

But suddenly the prospect scared her more than anything she'd ever encountered...up to and including her stint in the military.

Whatever had she left herself open for?

3

MAXINE PRIDED HERSELF on holding her own with the guys when it came to drinking. So she was really surprised that by the time the bar closed, she was feeling a little woozy. She couldn't remember having all that much to drink, but the way she was feeling told her that maybe she'd had one too many.

The girls had left a little earlier, smiling at her in a way that seemed to suggest they knew what was going to happen. Of course, that put them ahead of the game, because she wasn't all too sure what to expect, herself.

She caught sight of Jax moving in her direction and straightened in her chair. This so wasn't how she'd planned to feel during their first stretch of time alone together.

He, on the other hand, looked as actively hot as he had earlier in the evening. It was more than his thick shock of dark blond hair that always appeared in need of a comb, and his warm blue eyes that always made her think of summer skies and how much she craved the heat. He looked as if he was ready for anything and everything...especially a long, thorough roll in the hay.

Of course, his brief role playing Santa to all the girls in the place, including her and her friends, had left her feeling more than a little hot and bothered. She'd been so tongue-tied, she hadn't been able to tell him what she really wanted.

"You ready?" he asked.

It took her a moment to realize he was talking about the ride he was giving her to her aunt's house. Not her secret Santa wish. Damn.

"Oh. Yes." She smiled.

As he got their coats from behind the bar, she was aware of the bar owner's attention on them.

"Good night," she called.

"Good night, Maxi. Nice to see you again. Will you be back here tomorrow night?"

She waved noncommittally and led the way out.

The early morning air was still and cold. She couldn't remember a time she'd experienced such quiet. Perhaps because it contrasted so greatly with the riotous emotions roiling inside of her.

Her brief contact with Jax earlier, when she'd realized he wanted her—at least physically—left her breathless...and more than a little scared.

It was one thing to mentally decide on a course

of action; quite another, indeed, to actually embark on it.

She started toward where his truck was parked in the lot but found he wasn't behind her.

"I need to see to Cleo first," he said.

She stopped dead in her tracks. Cleo?

He grinned at her. "I rent the place above the bar."

"I don't understand. This is where you live?"

"Most nights. When I have a day off, I go out to Gram's, but this…" He gestured toward the wooden stairs leading up to a second story door. "This is my home away from home."

She followed him up. "And Cleo?"

"You're going to love her."

Max winced. She was sure whoever Cleo was, she was not going to love her. She'd hated everyone Jax had dated before. What would make this one any different? Especially since she appeared to live with him.

Double damn.

"Why did you agree to take me home if you weren't going that way?" she asked, trying to figure out what her options were. Truly, she'd preferred not to be stuck in a truck with him for a half hour if his heart already belonged to someone else.

"I haven't seen you in two years. Did you really expect me to say no?" He took keys out of his pocket and unlocked the door. "Besides, it's no big deal. I'll just crash at Gram's tonight."

A soft breeze brought the tang of his aftershave to her nose. She took a deep breath; she'd always loved the way he smelled.

He held out a hand to stay her. "You may want to step back for a minute while Cleo greets me."

Great. She was going to have to watch another woman throw herself into his arms.

He squared his stance and then opened the door. Max watched a female throw herself into his arms, all right. Or, rather, climb up into them.

She laughed as a black feline, more kitten than cat, climbed Jax like a tree, not stopping until she was safe in his arms and nudging her chin against his.

"Cleo," Jax said, "I want you to meet Max. Max..." He turned and smiled at her even as he scratched the cat behind the ears. "This is Cleo."

Max leaned forward, wondering if her relief was obvious, but not really caring. She was just happy Cleo wasn't a six foot blonde with model good looks she'd have to add to the top of her Most Hated list.

"Hey, Cleo," she said softly, holding her hand palm down so the cat could take a whiff of her. Then just as sweet as you please, Cleo rubbed up against the digits, her rumbling purr audible. Max ran her hand along her soft, warm fur.

"I would never have figured you for a cat person."

"I'm not."

Jax walked inside the apartment and Max followed. He switched on a light and closed the door behind them before placing the cat on the back of a chair.

"Long story short, Cleo is Gram's. She's just visiting while Gram takes a vacation."

"Vacation?"

He grimaced. "Yeah. She went on a cruise and won't be back until next week." He walked toward the back and switched on another light to what looked like the kitchen.

"I'm surprised she didn't leave her in the barn."

"Yeah, well, Cleo isn't a barn cat, exactly..." He adjusted what appeared to be a thermostat on the wall. "The heat shouldn't take but a minute."

"I'm fine. I've been through worse."

He looked at her. "Yeah. We both have, I think. Easy to forget that sometimes."

He disappeared into the other room. Max stared at Cleo who stared back, at least until she heard the sound of food hitting a bowl. Then she was off like a shot, skidding to a stop on the kitchen tile.

Max unzipped her leather jacket and looked around the place. Hell, it was neater than hers. And while the black, contemporary furnishings may have come with the place, the small touches did not. There were books in the case, a plant on the floor and photos in frames on the shelves. She stepped nearer, easily recognizing Jax's grandmother and brother Jason in the pictures. And then she spied one of herself...

Her heart skipped a beat as she picked up the simple four-by-six-inch frame of a photo shot taken about five years ago while they were serving together. They were both in desert fatigues and Jax had draped his arm casually over her shoulders.

There was nothing casual, however, about the way she smiled at him.

She squinted at her expression. How was it possible he never knew?

Then it occurred to her he had known. He just hadn't returned her feelings.

"Long time ago, huh?" he asked, coming to stand beside her.

"Huh?" She awkwardly put the frame back down. "Um, yeah. A different lifetime, it seems."

He ran his hand over his hair. "Yeah."

She stared into his face, wondering if she was just being stupid or if she'd been made that way. She started to ask if he was ready, when she noticed he'd taken off his coat, most likely leaving it in the kitchen.

"Maxi?"

"Huh?"

Jax grinned at her. "That's what Chuck called you back at the bar."

"Oh. Yeah." Was it her, or was it suddenly warmer in here?

"I'm surprised it didn't rate at least one of your famous sneers. It would have in the past."

She laughed, remembering all the names she'd been called in elementary school, Maxi Pad being by far the worst. She doubted she had to remind him of that, since he'd fought right alongside her a couple of times.

"That was until I was arrested for assault."

He lifted a brow.

"Joking. I'm joking." She shifted on her feet, noticing the way he looked at the front of her jacket as if trying to see what lay underneath. "People seem to prefer to call me Maxi…so I let them."

He didn't say anything for a long moment and then he cleared his throat. "It suits you."

"Yeah, well, that doesn't mean you get to call me that. I'm still Max to you. Try calling me anything else and you'll earn more than a sneer."

They both laughed, but as soon as the moment passed, she became all too aware that they were alone. Together. In his apartment. After midnight.

Her heart beat an irregular rhythm in her chest and she swore she could actually hear her blood rushing through her veins like water through a pipe. How dumb she'd been to think a tight pair of jeans and push-up bra would be enough to get his attention when nearly twenty years of clothing changes had not.

She ran her tongue over her dry lips. "I guess we'd better get going…"

Jax met her gaze solidly and didn't say anything for a long moment. She shoved her hands deeper into her jacket pockets and burrowed into the black leather.

"Listen, why don't you spend the night…" he said, his voice trailing.

She looked around nervously. There was only the one bedroom that she could see.

"The couch is a queen sleeper."

She turned back toward him.

"I know I told you I'd take you, and if you insist, of course, I will. But now that we're here and warm…"

Warm…

No, she was hot. Sweltering hot. And her state had nothing to do with the temperature outside.

"Here," he said. "Let me take your coat."

He reached to presumably help her take it off. She automatically started to shrug off the attention, then instead took a deep breath, turned and allowed him to help her.

Was it her, or did his fingers linger just that much longer at the nape of her neck? Skim down her arms when no contact was needed?

She swallowed thickly and swiveled back to face him, every inch of her yearning to feel him touch her more purposefully, more meaningfully, starting with a kiss…

"Max?"

Her name was little more than a whisper. Her gaze fell to his mouth, a mouth she'd seen a million times before, but had never so badly wanted to feel it against hers.

She was sure if he didn't kiss her right then and there she'd self-combust, leaving only the tiny particles that would scatter in the stiff winter breeze, leaving no hint she'd ever existed.

What scared her even more was that she was afraid the same might happen if he *did* kiss her…

4

JACKSON SWORE HE could still feel her hot bottom on his lap.

He grimaced and shifted uncomfortably, no longer wearing the Santa pants to hide the telltale signs of arousal. Her wiggling against him had left him far more turned on than he would ever have expected back at the bar. He wasn't sure he'd completely recovered from the moment.

Who was he kidding? The only thing responsible for his mental meanderings now was the sexy woman standing in front of him. Someone who had once been very familiar, but now seemed more like a stranger.

It didn't make any sense. Max had always been... well, Max. What in the hell had happened to her in the past two years to turn her into this tantalizing parcel of hotness?

One minute he'd been counting off the seconds

when his brief stint as Barracks' Santa would end and…the next, she'd stepped in front of him, hands on her curvy hips, and time had ground to a halt.

He'd had at least twenty women sit on his lap before her, not all of them innocently (Genie had wriggled so suggestively she'd nearly injured him). But the idea of letting Max climb on board had left him so tongue-tied, he'd barely been able to speak.

And now he'd just suggested she spend the night…

If he knew what was good for him, he'd grab his coat and drive her sweet bottom to her aunt's place. Now.

But at that moment he didn't care much about what was good for him. He was too focused on what he wanted. And right now, he wanted her…

She licked her full lips in the same way that had driven him to distraction earlier. He nearly groaned at sight of her pink tongue dipping out between her straight, smooth teeth, her actions causing the plump flesh to glisten.

"Are you sure this is a good idea…?"

The question was said so quietly, he nearly didn't hear it.

But he had…

And his answer was to do what he'd been wanting to all night: kiss her.

OH…SWEET…SALVATION…

The last thing Max expected was for Jax to kiss

her. She may have wanted it—wanted it? She craved it to the pads of her feet—but she'd somehow managed to convince herself that not only was he not interested in kissing her, he'd be offended if she kissed him.

Yet now his hot mouth pressed against hers, his tongue seeking entrance. Permission all too willingly granted.

Oh, yes…

His kiss was even sexier than she imagined it might be. And that was saying a lot considering she'd done a whole lot of imagining over the past decade and a half, her fantasy abilities growing with each chronological milestone she reached, every intimate experience she encountered.

This one kiss was better than all the kisses she'd ever enjoyed…combined.

What was that humming sound? Oh. It was her. And not only was she making strange, hungry noises, she was leaning into him…

Oh, was she ever leaning into him.

Max snaked her arms under his and made full-on contact, her fingers digging into the back of his denim shirt. If there had been any question of his physical awareness of her earlier, there was no mistaking it now: his hard length pressed insistently against her lower belly, telling her in no uncertain terms where he most wanted to be.

Exactly where she wanted him to be.

He caught her by the shoulders, as out of breath as she was. "Wait, wait, wait…"

She didn't want to wait. She'd waited long enough.

"This is…crazy…insane…"

She nodded. It was.

"Where did this come from? We've never…"

She was incapable of words. Hell, just then, she was incapable of breathing worth a damn.

"We're friends."

She smiled at that. "Yes, we are."

He was her best friend. The one person in the entire world she'd always known she could turn to if she needed anyone, someone to talk to about whatever was bothering her…

Until now. Now, she couldn't have uttered a word if she tried.

"I don't want…I mean, the last thing…"

He released her shoulders and she felt as if he'd just dropped her onto her face from a second story balcony.

She watched him pace away, then back again, running his hands through his hair again and again.

"This is nuts. We're friends. I don't want to lose that."

"Who says we have to?"

He stopped five feet away and stared at her. "Is this a good idea?" he asked, searching her face.

"I don't know," she whispered. "But it feels…"

Good? Phenomenal? Incredible?

She barely heard his groan before he placed his hands on either side of her face and kissed her again, this time within an inch of her life.

Yes…

Red-hot sensation swept over her, making her feel everything, yet nothing at all except a deep, needful hunger for his tongue against hers. She tunneled her fingers under his T-shirt, running them along his sides before curving them against his back, holding tight. So good, so right. So hot…

She gasped when she felt him slide his hands under her shirt, his knuckles grazing her stomach before he cupped both her breasts through her bra, then worked his way under it. As his thumbs rasped over her stiff nipples, fireworks erupted, unleashing a flood of emotion that weakened her bones, leaving her completely dependent on him to hold her upright.

He ripped his mouth from hers and bent his head, licking each of her nipples, squeezing her breasts just short of the brink of pain before drawing her right nipple deep into the hot depths of his mouth.

Max stretched her neck and moaned as he licked and sucked, the pool of need between her thighs deepening, widening, until she was sure she had creamed through her jeans.

She breathlessly cradled his head in her hands and drew him back up, kissing him hard, unable to get enough of him. He tasted, felt, smelled so good. Better than any one man had a right to.

Unable to stop herself, she slid her hand down between them, not stopping until she cupped the hard ridge of his sex under his jeans. She moaned at the thick length of him. Needing to feel more, she popped the steel buttons, not stopping until her fingers were inside his boxers and she held his throbbing flesh in her palm.

Oh, sweet hell…

She stroked him almost reverently, then squeezed, as if claiming possession.

His low groan fed her need.

As if he couldn't wait any longer, he opened the front of her jeans and pushed the denim over her hips, half taking her panties right with them. She stepped out of one leg and was about to step out of the other when he cupped her crotch, and stopped her breath.

He dragged his mouth from hers, his groan deeper. "God, you're so wet, so hot…"

Fingers sought and found access to the source of her heat. When his thumb grazed her clit, she bit on her bottom lip to keep from crying out. When that same thumb worked back and forth over her slick vagina, then thrust up deep inside her, she couldn't do anything but cry out, clutching his shoulders for dear life.

As she staved off orgasm with little hope of suc-

ceeding, she absently wondered why all this seemed
so new to her…so powerful. Surely, she'd known her
fair share of lovers, beginning with Johnny Denton
on the couch in the basement of his parents' house
just before her eighteenth birthday. Sure, the event
hadn't been anything memorable…and thankfully
she'd been curious enough to push on to her next
lover, determined to discover what everybody was
raving about.

But this…

This…

She cried out his name, coming so hard she was
sure the only thing supporting her was his hand and
the phenomenal things it was doing to her between
her legs.

"Oh my God…" she murmured again and again.

She kissed him lingeringly as he continued to
stroke her.

Then he grasped her womanhood solidly in his
hand. "I want you." His kiss gained momentum. "I
want to feel you, be inside you…"

Yes.

Max wasn't sure if she'd merely thought the word
or said it, but her response was unmistakable.

He backed her toward the bedroom and she went,
pushing back his denim shirt and tugging up his
T-shirt as they went, not finishing one before moving
onto the other while he did the same with her coat
and top and bra. They reached for each other's jeans

at the same time, fumbling until they gave up and did their own, hers still wrapped around one ankle as they tumbled to the bed.

Hurry, she wanted to whisper, before he changed his mind again.

Then, finally, he was sheathed and sliding into her to the hilt.

Max's back came up off the bed and her lungs seized, refusing air, a dark, throbbing heat diving deep, taking hold of her, making her tremble. She didn't think she'd ever known such a complete, utter connection with another human being. Until now. He filled her not only physically, but she felt inextricably joined with him in ways that transcended description.

He moved and a moan ripped from her throat from an untouched place she didn't recognize. It might have scared her if it were anyone else but Jax. But it was Jax. And he was all she'd ever need.

JACKSON HADN'T FELT the need to come so fast since he was a teen groping one of the Pearson twins in the cab of Gram's old Chevy truck.

No, not even then...

He took in the intoxicating expression of the woman under him thinking there was no way this could be his Max. Surely by now she should have batted him about the ears. Pushed him away and told him she was just joking.

But it was Max, and he was about to lose it totally...

Quick, what were the delay tactics he used to employ? Mentally disassembling his M-16 used to do the trick, but when he thought about his gun, all he could see was his thick shaft sinking into Max's sweet flesh inch by inch.

He grit his back teeth together and froze, his arms threatening to give out from under him where he held himself above her. Please don't let her move, please don't let her...

She moved.

Damn molten lava, he was going to lose it...

He did.

And there was absolutely no way he could disguise the fact that he did. The requisite groan, give-away stiffness and telltale jerking filled out the picture, putting him solidly back in that truck cab.

Only it wasn't a Pearson twin he was with, it was Max.

He collapsed against her, his face buried in the bedding over her shoulder, in a state of shock. Hell, she had to think him either a complete dork with no experience, or selfish beyond compare.

He felt her hands on his back, then heard her quiet giggle in his ear.

Jackson raised his brows as he slowly tested his arms and lifted himself back above her. Giggling? Max didn't giggle.

"Sorry," he mumbled.

Her smile was undeniable. "Don't be. I'm flattered."

She rubbed her ankles against the back of his calves, causing her slick muscles to contract as she did so. "Now if you were drunk, it would be another story altogether."

Damn, but she was beautiful. The Max he knew, as well as the one he was coming—quiet literally—to know. Her sense of humor disarmed his horror at his quick draw...and her subtle shifting worked wonders on other areas of his anatomy.

Testing himself, he slowly withdrew. But when she might have rolled out from under him, he replaced the condom and thrust back in to the hilt, satisfied at her gasp and the way she arched her back.

He waited a moment for her to open her eyes. When she did, his grin was what greeted her.

"What?" he asked, leaning in to kiss her. "You didn't think that was all there was?"

Her breasts trembled as he leaned in to take one of her pouty nipples into his mouth, then the other, swirling his tongue around the stiff nubs and then suckling them deeply, the control he was used to slipping gratefully back into place.

Oh, yeah. Now he was back on track. He kissed Max breathless and then stroked her both inside and out. This time he fully planned to be thorough about bringing her to orgasm, again and again and again...

5

MAX WAS SORE in places she hadn't known she had. But rather than frowning, she had to fight to keep from grinning. In the company of her mom and aunt, it wasn't wise to look too cheerful. They'd know something was up for sure and wouldn't stop until they uncovered what. And Max didn't plan to say anything to anybody about last night. Criminy, she was having a hard time convincing herself it had really happened…

It was midmorning and Jax had driven her home a few hours ago, well before her relatives had gotten out of bed so the story she told about Patience driving her home hadn't sounded any alarms. That was a good thing, because in the years she'd been away from home her mom and aunt had become even nosier than they'd been before, grilling her for details on every aspect of her life…up to and including sex. It was a new approach that had left her slack-jawed on more than one occasion since she'd returned home five days ago.

She sat at the old Formica kitchen table, running her fingertips over her extra large mug of coffee and staring through the window in the direction of the Savage farm. She couldn't see it from where she was sitting, but she gazed toward it anyway, wondering if Jax was up yet and whether or not he'd left to return to the city.

The old farmhouse Max grew up in had once belonged to her great-grandparents, who had built it plank by torturous plank (as her aunt told the story). Her aunt Theresa had inherited it twenty-five years ago, not without a little flack from family members, including Max's mom. But Theresa had stood fast and laid claim to the house as her inheritance, seeing to the upkeep and leasing out the surrounding land to local farmers to help toward the upkeep. Some people in town said it had cost her her marriage, but Max knew better. Of course, it didn't help that her cousins, Theresa's two adult children, bought into the rumors. It was more than the distance between Aunt Theresa and Denver that kept them from seeing each other more than once a month.

Max's mom Cindy had lived at the house on and off ever since she'd left Max's father twenty years ago, but mostly "on" for the past eight years, ever since Max had enlisted and been out on her own. Cindy had said she wanted to keep down expenses. Max suspected it was more for the company.

Cindy worked part-time at the feed/general store and part-time at the diner, while Theresa partially owned the only beauty shop in town and worked there. Neither of them left the house in the morning until they looked their "absolute best." You never knew when opportunity would come knocking (her aunt still told the story of a hunky UPS delivery man who showed up first thing one morning. She was convinced she'd missed out on the love of her life because she'd opened the door in her ratty bathrobe, her hair in curlers. The delivery man was said to have raced from the driveway so quickly, it had taken ten minutes for the gravel dust to settle).

The two women were the biggest reason why Max never really made an effort to look feminine...or anything except presentable for that matter. For one thing, she'd found it next to impossible to get into the bathroom, since one or the other of them was always in it. But mainly, she hadn't wanted to be like them. Over the years, she'd gone to great lengths to sabotage any of their attempts to dress her up when she was a teen by dyeing everything black and tearing stylish goth holes in anything she classified as "cute." Which was just about everything they'd ever bought for her.

Sometimes it seemed that all the two of them ever did was talk about their exes and how bad they'd had it, gossip about other people's love lives or gush about a guy they'd met, were dating or would like to date.

You'd think the sun rose and set on their romantic aspirations.

Max smiled and sipped her coffee, her mind sliding back to Jackson and last night. Wouldn't it be amusing if she discovered she wasn't really that different from her family after all?

"I know that smile," her aunt said, coming into the kitchen.

Both the words and her own thoughts nearly caused Max to choke.

Theresa poured herself a cup of coffee and then took the chair opposite her. Her mother looked up from where she was reading a gossip rag to her right.

"Well?" her aunt asked, not about to give up.

Max put her cup down. "You're the one who said you knew what it meant, so why don't you tell me? Because I haven't a clue what you're talking about."

Her mother folded the paper back to where she'd left off. "Oh, yes. You're right. How could I have missed it? Theresa, dear, I do believe our darling Maxine has gotten laid."

Holy shit!

Okay, time for her to go.

"Whose car do I get today?" Max asked, desperately trying to change the subject.

They exchanged a look and then a smile of their own Max wasn't sure she liked. Actually, she was positive she disliked it.

"What time are you going to be back?" her mom asked after offering her car.

"I don't know. I'm going into town to see about a job. Afterward, I'm checking into that truck Julie told me was for sale."

"No rush," her aunt said, watching her as she sipped her coffee.

"Where's the job?"

"I'll let you know if I get it," she said, hightailing it out of the room as quickly as possible. "See you later. Text if you need anything…"

She slammed the door on one of their responses, shrugging into her coat once she was outside and then closing her eyes and taking a deep breath of the frigid air. She'd wanted to shake off the aggravation brought on by having two overly curious women in her life. Instead, she found herself smiling again. Extra wide and likely much like a neon sign announcing what they'd seen: she'd gotten laid.

Only she hadn't merely gotten laid. She'd slept with Jackson Savage.

She tossed the car keys up into the air and caught them on the way to the nondescript sedan her mother drove, wondering when she might be able to sleep with him again…

JACKSON STEPPED OUTSIDE the front doors of Pegasus Security and blinked against the bright winter sun even as he took out his cell phone. Wasn't it ironic that on the heels of signing an employment contract with the rival of his brother Jason's company, his brother would call?

"Hey," he answered after deciding to accept it. He was due back inside in ten minutes for a meeting on an assignment he'd been given. "What's up? You still in town?"

"Yeah. I head out tomorrow. You want to have lunch?"

Jackson shot a glance over his shoulder at the squat building that looked like it had once been a warehouse and whose interior told him it hadn't been all that long ago.

"Sorry, can't."

"Why? What's up?"

Well, so much for sitting on the information for a while. "I just signed up with Pegasus."

"What? You can't be fucking serious?"

Jackson grimaced and paced away from the door when someone else came out. "Serious as a wart after a one-night stand."

The reference made him think of last night.

His brother filled his ear with profanity. "Yeah, well, quit. I don't like the thought of you working for that half-assed son-of-a-bitch."

"Yeah, well, you don't like the thought of me working for another half-assed son-of-a-bitch, either. That's exactly the reason I'm here."

"To prove a point?"

"No, to work in the profession of my choice."

"What's up with the bar?"

"Last night was the end. Slinging drinks at The Barracks wasn't exactly where I saw my career going. It was only a stopgap measure until you came to your senses."

"You could have owned that joint. Turned it into a restaurant—"

"Look, I'm not in the mood to hash all this out with you again…"

The sun glinted off the windshield of an old sedan pulling into a spot some twenty-five feet away. He watched as Max got out.

Holy shit.

He grimaced. "Look, I've got to go. Have a nice trip back to Baltimore tomorrow. Tell Jordan I said hey."

His brother started to argue but Jackson pressed the disconnect button and pocketed the cell, watching as Max walked toward Pegasus. He squinted at her, feeling even more confused. The way she looked now, well, this was the Max he remembered—hair back, face devoid of makeup, loose-fitting khaki and flack jacket the name of the game.

Outside of a couple of obvious differences, she looked like one of the guys.

He swallowed hard, remembering that last night she'd been anything but.

Oh, hell, was he ever in trouble…

He knew the instant she realized it was him standing there. Her face lit up in that way it always did, but his reaction to it was vastly different.

"Hey," she said, stopping in front of him.

"What are you doing here?"

His words were out before he had a chance to check them.

She laughed. "You told me last night that this place was hiring. Remember?"

Oh, hell, he had, hadn't he?

He not only remembered passing on the word at the bar when she asked if there were any job openings, but had held no qualms about doing so.

Until now.

"What's wrong?" she asked.

Her smile disappeared. He discovered he was fixated on her mouth, remembering something else entirely. Like how mind-blowingly fantastic it had been to kiss it.

"Nothing."

She gestured toward the door. "You going in?"

"Yeah."

He motioned for her to precede him in, wondering why in the hell he had never noticed her ass looked so damn good in khaki...

Then he realized he had noticed. He just hadn't thought he'd ever have a chance to taste it.

Good Lord, what had he gotten himself into?

He caught the door she opened. The bigger question was how in the hell he was going to get himself into it again, and again...

6

MAX HAD NO SOONER walked onto the premises than a confidentiality agreement and employment contract were being thrust at her, and she was being ushered into a room with fifteen others to be briefed on an assignment.

The quickness didn't allow her the time she craved to digest Jax's reaction when she approached the building. He'd appeared pleased, giving wings to what seemed like birds in her stomach...then one flew up into her throat when she thought she'd seen disappointment in his eyes. While she hadn't expected a hug and hot kiss...well, some sign that last night had happened would have been nice.

Something, anything other than disappointment...

Now, she tried to focus her attention on the man at the front of the room. She'd been introduced to Lenny Storehouse and welcomed aboard. Jax stood somewhere behind her, but she forced herself not to look. Truth was, she was afraid of what she might see reflected on his face.

She didn't have a notepad on her so she paid close attention to what the team leader was saying. Problem was, the forty-something guy with a crew cut didn't seem to be making much sense.

Was he really suggesting a transport would be taking them all to coastal Africa within a few hours?

Oh, she was confident in her own abilities, and knew she was up for the job—which was briefly outlined as a covert military operation to aid in the recovery of three Navy Seals who had been taken captive, along with the targets they'd been sent in to retrieve (a vacationing retired couple with ties to the first family who had been taken hostage by pirates)—but there was no way Pegasus could know that about her with little more than a scan of her resume. Not a single call had been made, not one fact check performed.

She looked around her. What did that say about the others in the room? Most appeared to be around her age, save for two or three who might be in their thirties. All of them faced forward, looking a little too confident for comfort.

Jax stepped to her other side. "This guy is a whack job."

She forced herself not to look at him. "I'm afraid evidence is weighing in that direction, yes."

"Recruit? You have something you want to share

with the room?" the drill sergeant wannabe stopped his monologue and asked her.

"Sir, no sir," she said.

Jax cleared his throat. "Actually, I have a question if we've reached that portion of the briefing."

"We have."

"Who'll be leading the team?"

"I will."

"Shit," he said under his breath so only Max could hear. "How long have the other recruits been employees of the company?"

Max found everyone in the room looking at them.

"As long as they need to be. Are you questioning my qualifications as team leader, Savage?"

Max looked at her boots. Hell, *she* was. This was a private company, not a branch in the military. In the Marines, she'd not only trained with her fellow soldiers, she knew they were at least as capable, if not more so, than her. She trusted she could count on them as much as they count on her.

She looked around the room. She didn't even know the names of these people...

"No, sir," Jackson said. "I'm not. Merely looking to educate myself."

The two men stared at each other and Max resisted the urge to roll her eyes at the dick-measuring contest.

"Anyone else?" Lenny asked, turning toward the rest of the group.

There were a couple of questions about gear and end game.

"Good, if there isn't anything else…"

"Life insurance?" Jackson called out.

Brushhead glared at him. "It's explained in the employment agreement."

"It's thirty days before it goes into effect. Which means that if something happens now…well, families see nothing."

There was some conversational noise in the room, as Max suspected there would be.

Holy hell. Were all of them new recruits?

She met Jackson's gaze. It was a smart way to uncover the information as well as point out an important caveat.

"Reasonable compensation should match risk factor," Jackson said to Lenny.

"Second," a recruit called out.

"Third," said another.

The room went silent.

Finally, Lenny said, "Fine. Papers on full benefits will be prepared for you to sign before the transport leaves. Dismissed."

They began filing from the room, Max and Jackson bringing up the rear. Once they were in the hall, he grasped her arm.

"I want you out of here."

She blinked at him. "What?"

"I have to be here, but you don't. Go to Jason's place—Lazarus. You'll get a job there, no problem."

"Why aren't you working there?"

"Question of the day."

"I'm not following you."

"It's a long story. And it doesn't matter right now. What does, is you need to get out of this place as fast as your boots will carry you."

She squared her shoulders. "I signed a commitment."

"That they won't enforce."

"What? You don't think I'm up for the job?"

Lenny came out of the room, paused slightly to glare at Jackson, then continued down the hall.

"No, Max...I don't think they're up for the job."

"Then come with me."

He didn't say anything for a long moment.

He was so handsome, she thought, taking in his intense expression. His dark blond hair needed a trim but was combed back neatly, tempting her fingers. His deep blue eyes were clear and heart-stoppingly beautiful, even given the steely determination they now held. His mouth...

She swallowed thickly.

"I can't," he said.

Max cleared her throat and looked away, searching for the thread of their conversation she'd apparently dropped.

"Well, I can't, either."

She began to turn and he grasped her arm again.

Her heart skidded to a stop at the touch that was everything but intimate.

"What's with the brotherly concern all of a sudden, Savage?" she asked, purposely using his surname. "I don't recall you ever trying to push me out of the way before."

He blinked.

She was glad, because it meant he was considering her words.

"Look," she continued. "I've never backed out of an obligation in my life. And I'm not going to start now. So you might as well get it through your thick head I'm not going anywhere. And if you feel you can't trust me…"

Her voice caught slightly on the last two words, startling her. Thankfully, he didn't seem to notice.

"If you feel you can't trust me, well, then I suggest you stay away from me."

He searched her face. "Hell, Max, you're probably the only one here I *do* trust. That is the reason I'd prefer you weren't here."

"Yes, well, I am. Get used to it."

He dropped his hand.

"Now if you'll excuse me, there are some arrangements I need to make. I'm sure the same applies to you. I'd just as soon be as prepared as possible for this trip."

He nodded.

"Catch up with you later," she said.

"Yeah. Later."

She began to turn when she caught a glint in his eyes.

"What?" she demanded.

His sexy grin provided air under the bird wings in her belly. "Did I say anything?"

She couldn't help smiling back at him. "Nope. That's just as well. Because if you tried to stop me again, I would have been forced to coldcock your stubborn ass."

She turned and stalked down the corridor, his chuckle sending tiny bumps running up and down her arms.

Why did she get the feeling this assignment wasn't going to resemble anything she'd ever encountered before? Oh, boy...

7

JACKSON ATTEMPTED TO relax against the straight-backed seat positioned against the inside of the transport. While it was reassuring they were being taken to their assignment destination in a military plane, he still didn't feel all that comfortable with his team members...or the team leader.

After Max left Pegasus's premises following the meeting earlier in the day, presumably to drive out to her aunt's and make arrangements to be gone for what was expected to be at least a five-day trip, he'd stayed behind, his intention to insert himself into more of a position of authority. Whether it was due to his solid resume, or the urgency of the operation, or the two combined, he'd easily accomplished his goal.

So going in, he and Lenny Storehouse would be co—team leaders, with Storehouse taking the ultimate lead. Then Jackson had gone about getting to know as much about his team as he could.

THE MOB. That was the acronym he'd assigned the members he'd chosen: Taylor-Hershey-Evans-Max-O'Selznick-Bachman, with the *O* being added by the recruit when he'd introduced himself. "David O. Selznick," he'd said. With his close-cropped red hair it would be easy to remember him as an *O'* something.

Taylor was a single mother of two and former Army Infantry. Hershey was a Hispanic male, Navy. Evans was a farm-fed cowboy with a country accent and was a former Ranger, while Bachman had longish hair and looked like he played in a rock band... which, Jackson had discovered, he did: bass. Something his Marine superiors hadn't much liked.

Max, of course, was easy to remember and was an automatic: her name made up the *M* in the acronym.

He'd chosen the five because of their solid military backgrounds and dispositions, not because of their initials. The additional eight team members reminded him of guys he'd seen in Marine boot camp, when he'd pretty much guessed which of his fellow recruits would make it through, and which would be going home.

He couldn't be sure what the other members' military backgrounds were, though he hoped they had at least minimal experience in the service. Still, he was pretty much convinced most of the eight would have gone home within the first week of boot camp. That didn't bode well for him and Max when it came to backup. Hell, he didn't plan on depending on THE MOB unless it was absolutely necessary when it came to that.

But these others…

He glanced at where one of the younger guys had just barfed into the helmet Pegasus had provided, apparently airsick, then looked beyond him to where four more played poker, their shouts over the loud drone of the engines grating. The other three stayed apart from the rest, one sleeping, the other two attached to their cell phones either madly texting or browsing Facebook; he didn't know, didn't care.

He glanced at where Max sat next to him, watching as she took in their teammates with the same professional detachment. She grimaced. He nodded.

They'd been in the air for about two hours. He estimated they had at least ten more to go, allowing for a stop for refueling. That would make it roughly the middle of the night to these guys; middle of the day for where they were heading. And given the hostile environment, he suspected they would have to hit the ground running.

He glanced at Lenny Storehouse, their fearless operations leader, where he lay back with his cap tilted down over his eyes. He had the right idea, at least. It was important to get as much shut-eye as possible now, because nobody knew how much they were going to see later.

He reached up for his own cap and worked it down to shield his eyes. After a few moments, he cracked his eyes open to look at Max. She'd either already followed suit or beaten him to it. Hell, given the way her full mouth was slightly open, he suspected she was already asleep.

Of course, they really hadn't gotten a whole hell of a lot of it the night before, had they?

"What you looking at, Marine?" she said just loud enough for him to hear.

"Nothing. Nothing at all."

"Good. Go to sleep."

"Yes, ma'am."

She kicked his boot without opening her eyes.

"I mean, sir."

She laughed at that and then settled in more comfortably, crossing her arms under her full breasts.

Jackson's mouth watered with the desire to taste one of the pert nipples that lay under that nondescript cotton.

If he wasn't mistaken, her breathing had grown shallower. He looked up to find her watching him from beneath the thick fringe of her lashes.

"Done?" she asked, arching a brow.

He grinned. "Not nearly."

She smiled and then closed her eyes again.

He did the same, allowing himself to entertain ideas of what he'd like to do with her when they were back home and he had her alone again...

MAX SWALLOWED HARD. As far as signs of life went, the one Jax had just given her sent the needle soaring off the charts.

Okay, maybe not quite to that degree, but given the cool detachment he'd demonstrated toward her earlier...well, his naughty grin and the way he'd visually inhaled her breasts was enough to make her blood hum.

So he wanted her. That was good, right? She twisted her lips and readjusted the bill of her cap. Considering the alternative, it was definitely good.

Then why did she want him so much she ached on the one hand, yet, on the other, she was scared to death that he was only interested in sex?

Made no sense, did it?

She quietly cleared her throat and tried to clear her mind along with it.

Earlier she'd called her mom and aunt and made arrangements for them to bring her gear halfway, then for her mom to drive her back into town. She hadn't told Cindy exactly what her new job entailed, just that she'd be out of touch for a few days.

"But why do you need so many...guns?"

There weren't that many, she'd pointed out. Just three: one 9mm Beretta, one 10mm Colt and a fully automatic M-16.

But to someone who had no interest in firearms except for the shotgun they always kept around the farmhouse, she supposed the three represented an entire arsenal.

Cindy had hugged her so hard she couldn't breathe after they'd pulled up in Pegasus's parking lot. "You've just now come home. I don't want to lose you again."

Max had been surprised and touched by the words, which surprised and touched her, since it hadn't been all that long ago that she'd have given an eye roll at such sentiments.

She couldn't quite figure out what made this visit home different than previous ones. She was still the same person. Nothing significant had happened to make her view her surroundings or her family any differently.

Well, that wasn't entirely true...

Still, she found herself needing to reassure her mother in a way she never had before. So she'd returned the tight hug, waiting it out until its natural conclusion instead of eagerly ending it, afraid of what others might think if they saw her, wary that the moment might be viewed as weakness by her team members.

In that one moment, the only thing that mattered was her mother...and Max's need to soothe her fears.

"You're not losing me," she said. "I'll be back next week."

She only hoped she was right. She'd never worried much about how her assignments and the possible outcomes—her being injured or worse—might affect her family. Now, though...

Well, now she shifted uncomfortably and squashed the desire to take in her team members again. They weren't going to inspire any more confidence than they had five minutes ago.

But it was more than that. For reasons she wasn't presently equipped to understand, somehow the value of her life had increased. Not only in terms of awareness of what her loss might mean to her mother and aunt, but...

She held her breath briefly, realizing she wanted to see where this—the bubbling newfound emotions she felt for Jax—were going.

She wanted to live to know more than his touch and his friendship.

She felt his knee brush against hers ever so slightly and looked to see if he was sleeping. She couldn't tell. Was the physical move unconscious? Or had it been made to help ease her mind?

Little did he know that his mere presence did that. Jackson Savage was as good as it got when it came to combat situations.

What was she talking about? Jackson Savage was as good as it got when it came to anything.

She could almost imagine herself lying naked across his bed, cradling him between her thighs, her stomach quivering, his hot breath against her neck, his hard, long length filling her to overflowing. How long had they gone at it? Three hours? Four? And she easily believed they could have gone hours longer if not for the thought of her aunt and mom waking to find her bedroom empty.

Her nipples hardened and the crotch of her panties dampened at the thought of what lay ahead.

And what did lie ahead? A series of one-night stands? Hot ones? Or was it possible they could mold their newfound physical desire for each other with their longstanding friendship and…

What?

She wasn't thinking marriage, was she? Kids? White picket fence?

In her meandering thoughts on the matter, she hadn't allowed any of them to travel quite that far down the road. At this point, she was having problems seeing beyond the next five seconds, much less years.

Still, she couldn't ignore the deep thrumming of her heart at the idea of happily-ever-after with Jax.

Just think of all the red-hot sex they could spend the next fifty years having.

Damn…

She readjusted her cap again, a thousand hot and erotics thoughts coming to her at once. She fought them off one by one, concentrating instead on the hum of the engines, the cadence of her heartbeat, the thrum of her pulse...

Finally, her mind surrendered to what her body needed most: sleep.

And to her dreams...

8

Here we go...

As Jackson predicted, nearly ten hours later the plane was positioned over the landing site and the team was lined up to jump out the back lip that had been opened. Max stood in front of him, three back from the lead. He stifled the desire to tuck her behind him and ground his back teeth together. He really needed to get over this new need of his to protect her.

"Go! Go! Go!" the team leader shouted.

The first member seemed frozen to the spot. The second member didn't so much urge him forward, as shove him out.

Great...

Within moments, Jackson was freefalling, homing in on the target zone outlined an hour before on a map by Lenny. It was a small clearing near an easily identifiable waterfall. Protective goggles in place, he

glanced to his right to find Max pulling her ripcord.
He followed suit. The plane had dropped them at a
lower altitude so their descent would be quick and
not so easily tracked. Within moments, he released
the chute and hit the ground rolling to prevent injury,
relieved when Max landed twenty feet away, doing
the same. They quickly gathered their chutes and
stashed them under some brush along the tree line
even as team members hit the ground behind them.
He watched as Max snatched one of the younger
guys out of the way of another coming even as one of
the other guys got caught in the higher branches of
a tree. He released the chute and fell to the ground.
Jackson winced. That had to hurt.

He helped the man to his feet. "Got it?"

He nodded.

To his satisfaction, the team he'd put together
immediately assembled. The others hung back and
walked around as Storehouse consulted his GPS.
The chute on top of the tree was camo but it would
still be easily identifiable by air. Which made it that
much more important for them to hightail it out of
there now.

"This way. Go! Go! Go!"

As planned, Max took the lead and Jackson
brought up the rear, with their team closely inter-
twined with the other. The guy who fell hard was
limping and slowing things up, as was the one who'd
suffered airsickness. He shouted them on.

They had seven klicks to go before they reached the designated area where they would stop to establish base camp. And in this hot, tropical environment, it was already destined to be a long seven klicks. With these guys, it was going to be even harder...

MAX SET A DRIVING, even speed, sweat covering her face. Hard to believe it wasn't all that long ago she could make a fifty-mile hike with over a hundred pounds of gear on her back and never blink an eye.

They said civilian life made you soft. She hadn't believed that until now. She was laboring harder than she should have been. After two years out of the service, it was almost like she'd never been in it.

She was almost relieved when the radio crackled and Lenny told her to cut her pace in half.

She readily agreed, turning to see only two others had kept pace with her.

Well, it wasn't as if she hadn't kept active. She made it to the gym at least four times a week for a grueling workout that was at least equivalent to what she'd done in the service. And her jobs had been ones that required she stay in shape (bodyguard, high-end security for visiting diplomats), but it had been a few years since she'd seen this kind of action...and her body was letting her know it.

Maybe it was the tropical environment. She was used to the desert. Heat she could take, but this humidity seemed to weigh on her more heavily than her gear. She knew they were heading closer to the coast. Hopefully the sea winds would help negate the humidity levels. She could hope, anyway.

She swiped at her brow with her wristband and glanced over her shoulder to find the rest of them had almost caught up. Good. She caught sight of Jackson's grin. She turned back to the front, her grin spreading across the whole of her face. His approval gave her a pair of fresh feet. She easily made it the seven klicks without seeming winded.

She drew to a halt and turned, waiting as everyone caught up.

"Christ, McGuire, you training for the Olympics?" Lenny asked. "Okay, everyone. Take five and let's get this done…"

JACKSON WASN'T SURPRISED when he and Max were two of the four chosen to walk the perimeter when night fell. After the fast-paced hike, most of the team had collapsed where they stood, trying to catch their breath. Hours later, they'd barely moved.

So here he was, facing four hours of perimeter duty in the dark in unfamiliar territory. Which is exactly the way he liked it.

There were few things that got the blood pumping like being on the front line. His senses seemed more aware, more alert. He'd come to understand that you never felt more alive than when you were in the path of possible death.

He'd walked his stretch of the perimeter three

times, taking notice of particular landmarks and most likely approach paths, more comfortable with his surroundings. He heard a quiet voice on his radio.

Max.

He picked it up.

"Fallujah," she said.

"Roger, that."

He switched to channel 69, the one they'd designated back when they'd served in Iraq to talking privately. He hesitated before speaking, the number just now registering to him. He smiled and lifted the radio to his mouth.

"What took you so long?" she asked, her voice quiet.

"Was just noticing the number…"

There was a pause then, "Yeah. Made me stop for a minute, too. Funny, huh? We used it so long without really thinking about it…"

He leaned against a tree, his gaze alert as he kept an eye out. They'd had a good laugh about it in the beginning, choosing the number because of its ease in remembering.

Now…

Jackson's mouth watered as he recalled the way she tasted, hardened as he practically felt her tongue against his erection…

Damn. The last thing he should be thinking about right now was oral sex…

"You still there?" he asked.

"Yeah. All quiet."

"Here, too." He put the radio to his chest then lifted it again. "You remember the first time we did this?"

She indicated she did.

He smiled.

"We were in separate transports on the Highway of Death. Fifty miles of a whole lot of nothing except for people wanting to kill us…"

"And everyone else was asleep."

He watched a moth-sized mosquito land on his forearm. He let it, then flexed his muscles, watching it get stuck and pop.

"That's the first time you told me about your dad," he said.

Silence. He knew she was remembering the conversation just as he was.

Claude McGuire had been an asshole of a man. A wife beater and deadbeat who couldn't keep a job to save his life. How her mother had handled it for all those years was beyond either of them. Thankfully, the first time he raised his hand to six-year-old Max, Cindy was out of there.

He couldn't imagine what might have happened otherwise.

Throughout their childhood, she hadn't said much about her dad. Mostly, she went quiet whenever he inquired, giving a shrug and a quiet, "You know…"

But he hadn't known. He couldn't have begun to imagine. He'd assumed the man had taken up with another woman or some other such thing.

But that quiet night on the radio in Iraq, Max had finally shared the truth with him.

"I remember. At the time, he'd just written to me," she said. "Surprised the hell out of me. Hadn't heard from him in nearly fifteen years."

Jackson grimaced, remembering the son-of-a-bitch had actually asked her for money.

"Did you ever write back to him?" he asked.

"No."

He couldn't blame her.

"I still wonder if I made the right decision."

"Whatever decision you make is always the right one."

He could envision her mulling that one over. "I still remember what you said."

He grimaced, checked his M-16 and scanned the area again.

"You know, about your willingness to give anything to see your dad again…"

He was afraid she'd remember that. "That was before you told me everything."

"Yeah, but people change. And there was that picture…"

He hadn't seen it then, the photo in question. But she had shown him back at the base that morning. It was a standard grade elementary school shot of a ten-year-old girl with a grin that showed teeth too big for her tiny face. Max's half-sister.

"Did you ever tell your mother?" he asked quietly. "You know, that he contacted you?"

"No."

He nodded.

"Hey," she said. "Whatever happened to that girl you were dating back then? You know, the one with the fake knockers?"

His responding chuckle caught him off guard. Not good. He told her he was going to go silent for a few minutes then switched back to the main channel. All was good and twenty yards later, all was still clear.

He switched the radio back on. "They weren't fake."

"Uh-huh."

"Trust me, I know the difference."

He pictured her giving one of her infamous eye rolls. "Right."

"Anyway, she wasn't my girlfriend. She was just a girl I was dating before I left."

"Ditzy Diane," she said. "I remember now."

He grinned at the nickname everyone had given her after she'd knitted a sweater for him two sizes too big and sent it to him…in the middle of summer with temps soaring to 110 in the shade.

"Yeah, not exactly the brightest bulb on the string," he admitted.

"Good thing you weren't dating her for her brains, huh?"

"They were real."

"Uh-huh."

"Anyway," he said quietly, "yours beat out hers any day."

Silence.

"Max?"

"What?"

"You still there?"

"Obviously."

"Trying to come up with a smart-ass response?"

He heard the smile in her "Yeah."

"Not getting anything?"

"No."

"Good."

She laughed. "I think it's about time for check-in. Talk later?"

He could spend the rest of his life talking to her.

The thought caught him up short and he stopped in his tracks.

"Out," she said.

He lifted the radio to his mouth but she'd already switched channels…

9

HOURS LATER, Jackson met Max and the crew at base camp. It was time to go. They had an easy five-klick hike to their destination to free the two civilian hostages and the three Navy Seals who had been taken captive on a previous failed rescue attempt. Once this was over with, they'd meet their transport out at 0500 hours.

He glanced over at Max in her camo gear and felt ridiculously turned on. The girl was hot. And he liked knowing he was the only one who knew exactly how hot.

Okay, maybe he had thought of her in that way from time to time over the years, had unconsciously indulged in a wet dream or twenty. Woken up drenched in sweat, his cock throbbing, his thoughts full of her. But seeing as they were friends, and Max would have just as soon sucker punched him as kiss him, there'd been no danger of anything happening before.

Now…

Well, now he found it curious the word *danger* entered the equation anywhere. And not just in their current physical situation in the middle of an African rain forest. Jackson had always known Max wasn't the kind of girl a guy could love and leave. Not that he'd any interest in that before.

But now?

"Same formation as before," Lenny said, interrupting his thoughts in a not altogether unwelcome way. Best he not think about Max as forever material now. "Go! Go! Go!"

Max took off at an easy jog and the others lined up after her. For an unreasonable moment, he felt the urge to object: he wanted to trade places with Max.

He grimaced as he brought up the rear. Where did those thoughts keep coming from? In some profound way he was incapable of working out just then, everything had changed. She wasn't just Max anymore, she was something else. And the undeniable desire he had to protect her grew with every breath he took. If something happened to her…

Ten minutes into the hike, he heard a crack to his right.

He automatically pushed the guy in front of him forward, then dropped to a crouch, his M-16 instantly in front of him as he scanned the surrounding trees.

"Nine o'clock!" he shouted.

Everyone scrambled, taking cover.

He switched on the night scope and honed in on the subject. It was an African national half hidden behind a tree, his own weapon aimed at someone other than Jackson. The guy wore what looked like old fatigues from which the arms had been raggedly cut, along with the legs. He focused on the face: hell, he was a kid. No more than fifteen or sixteen at most.

Jackson knew this area was filled with kid-populated militias run by warlords who didn't give two cents worth of thought to protecting their men. There were plenty of poverty-stricken boys just like this one hungry for a square meal and attention.

Jackson also knew not to underestimate the boy. The kid would kill him just as soon as look at him.

Damn.

Was the shooter alone? He couldn't tell. Now that the targets had scattered and no clear shot was to be had, Jackson scanned one-hundred-and-eighty degrees, then shifted on his feet to scan the area to his right. It looked like the kid was alone, which might explain why he hadn't squeezed off a shot yet. He was probably doing what Jackson was: namely, taking stock of the situation, counting the number in their team, gauging risk and success.

Had he called in their location? He couldn't see a radio, but although it was best to prepare for the worst and hope for the best.

How far away might reinforcements be?

Gauging his own risks, he took aim…and shot, the crack reverberating through the forest and startling slumbering wild life.

He watched in his scope as the target fell. He'd aimed for a flesh wound to the shoulder, something that would take the kid down and hurt like hell, but wasn't fatal.

He dashed the twenty yards to the target. In the light from the half moon filtering through the trees, he saw that the boy's face was contorted in pain and he desperately gripped his right shoulder…but it didn't stop him from reaching for his weapon.

Jackson grabbed the gun, looking at the old rifle that could probably produce a good shot at close range, but would likely have been worthless for anything else.

He emptied it of ammo and threw the gun one way, the rounds the other, then checked the boy for a communication device. Nothing. Good.

"He's still alive."

Jackson considered where John, one of Lenny's men, had come up beside him, his M-16 pointed directly at the kid's head.

Jackson reached out and moved John's weapon away. "I missed. He'll probably die of the wound anyway. Why don't you get back to the line and radio in the all clear?"

John stared at him, then at the kid. "We should finish him off."

"He'll suffer more this way."

John squinted at him. "You sure?"

His response was an unwavering stare.

"Fine. Let me know if you change your mind."

He made so much noise getting back to the path, Jackson wanted to shout at him to be quiet.

He glanced back at the kid's face: he was more hurt than scared.

He bent over, ripped a length of material from the hem of his shirt, then tucked it under where the boy's hand was gripping the wound. A glance at the front and back showed the bullet had gone right through, as intended.

"Here," he said, pushing the kid's hand down on the fabric. "Hold tight."

He muttered something in his native tongue Jackson didn't understand. Jackson patted him on the other shoulder then rose to his feet.

"Clear!" he shouted.

He heard Lenny over the radio shout for double time, apparently having come to the same conclusion he had—even though the kid hadn't called in their location, there was no telling where the rest of his group was. And there was always the chance someone had heard the gunshot and were even now on their way.

As he jogged to catch up with the line, Jackson tried to catch sight of Max, but she was too far ahead. Damn...

MAX LEANED IN with the rest of the team to take in the map Lenny had stretched out on the ground. He quietly outlined the target compound located some two hundred and fifty meters away on the other side of a crumbling and recently reinforced wall. Once the home of the ousted president of the third-world, conflict-ridden country, it had long since been taken over by one of the most powerful warlords in the region, serving as but one of his command centers. Thankfully, intelligence showed he wasn't currently staying there. Instead it was being used by one of his commanders and was the place where the recovery targets were being held captive.

"Are we to rendezvous with Corps troops already in place?"

Max looked across the circle to where Jax had asked the question.

Lenny rolled up the map. "No."

"It was my understanding—"

"Understand this, Savage—plans change. But this one remains the same. We're going in to get those targets out."

Silence reigned as the group stared at Jackson; it

appeared they were questioning his sanity when they should be questioning that of their leader.

Max stretched the tight kinks out of her neck. In the service, you were taught to follow. That was easy. Then again, the leaders were worthy of the honor.

Out here, in the private sector...well, while she didn't have much to base her doubts on, neither did she know enough to feel comfortable putting complete faith in the man who'd essentially just dressed down Jax for insubordination.

"We need to tighten the circle," Jax said next to her.

She looked at him in the dark. His eyes were luminous in the dim moonlight. He was so handsome she had trouble breathing. She nodded.

They had fifteen minutes to regroup before they advanced. They'd been given a crude layout of the main house inside the wall, along with two guesthouses, guard shack and storage units. The sleeping quarters of the main house was where their targets were being held.

Jackson brought together his team. Max had to agree with his choices; the five of them were by far the most competent of the group. The team listened intently, asked intelligent questions, were clear-eyed and focused. The others... She looked around. The others were in various states of distraction, stretching, running in place, trying to cover the fear they were so obviously experiencing, allowing it to control them instead of asserting control over it.

She glanced at Storehouse who spoke on a satellite phone phone, wondering who he was talking to and whether or not it had anything to do with backup should they need it.

"BEST HS." That was the acronym she'd given to the team based on their names.

"What?" Jax had said incredulously when she'd shared the tidbit with him back at camp.

"Bachman-Evans-Savage-Taylor-Hershey-Selznick," she'd explained.

"And you?"

"What's your shortcut?" she'd asked instead of answering.

"THE MOB."

"No *S*."

"Nope."

"Selznick?"

"O'Selznick."

She'd laughed. "Well, you didn't include yourself either…"

Fifteen minutes later, their team within a team was set.

"Go! Go! Go!" Lenny called.

Max and Jackson went out first, as agreed, leading two-by-two with the only other female on their team, Taylor, bringing up the rear. One of Storehouse's cockier rogue team members pulled out in front of them, doing his best impression of Rambo, while she noticed the others were perfectly content hanging back and allowing Jackson's team to go ahead.

They reached the seven-foot wall. Max instantly picked up on sound: it appeared at least two men were talking on the other side.

She held up her hand to halt advance and to indicate they should split up and move farther down the wall in opposite directions. Unfortunately, Braden, aka Rambo, had other plans.

"Screw this…"

He scaled the wall.

Max stared at Jackson and they both hustled fifteen feet on either side of Braden's position and then scaled to perch on top of the wall.

Automatic gunfire broke out. Max grit her teeth as she watched rounds disappear up Braden's flack jacket and undoubtedly through his vest below. Then he took a couple to the head. She flinched as he slumped over and then fell over the wall.

It all happened within a blink and there'd been nothing she and Jax could do.

Now, however, was different story…

She opened up fire and so did he, taking out the two guards with minimal trouble.

Damn.

Damn, damn, damn!

She gave the all clear to the men behind her and then jumped to the compound grounds.

Just in time to watch what looked like an entire battalion file out of a nearby building, weapons at the ready...

10

IT WAS A CLUSTERFUCK, pure and simple...

The instant they hit the ground, all hell broke loose. The compound had been much better manned than they'd been led to believe. Militia emerged from every shadow and appeared prepared for their arrival.

For a brief, paralyzing moment, all Jackson could think of was Max... He battled his way to cover, knowing there was nothing he could do for her if he was no longer there to do it.

Now, five agonizingly long minutes later, he hunched down behind a crude circle of stones that served as a water well, his M-16 reloaded and ready. He immediately spotted where Max was, standing across from him flat against the wall of an outdoor shower.

He knew such a flood of relief he took an unprecedented moment to close his eyes and send up a prayer of thanks. She was okay…

When he looked at her again, he found her face communicated the same sense of relief at finding him alive.

He didn't know what he'd do if he lost her now that he felt he'd just finally found her…

The thought alone was nearly paralyzing, not merely because of the physical threat the distraction posed but the emotional one.

Focus, Savage…

He scanned the area around him, taking in the situation. He couldn't be sure where his other team members were, or how many had survived the initial counterattack.

Shit. What an unqualified mess.

He couldn't help thinking they'd been sent in there like sacrificial lambs. Nothing was as it had been outlined. Intelligence was bad. And he was afraid the reason why the compound was so heavily fortified was because the warlord, the number one guy, was in residence, not one of his commanders, as they'd been told.

He'd learned early on in his career there were two things you needed in order to succeed in any mission: capable soldiers and accurate intelligence.

And they had neither. Yes, it was a clusterfuck. Pure and simple.

The question was, how were he and Max going to survive it?

He steeled himself and looked over the well wall, gauging the situation, then quickly ducked back down without incident. Five guards to the left, three to the right. He looked to see Max doing the same. Their gazes met. Then they both nodded.

They swung around at the same time, aiming and firing before taking cover again.

Two to the left, none to the right...

Max motioned that she was coming to him. He stood and delivered cover fire, taking out the remaining two.

Unfortunately, there were at least ten others somewhere on the compound...and those were only the ones he knew about. He could only hope none of them were behind them.

"This is messed up," Max said, crouching next to him.

"Agreed." He checked his radio: silent. Attempts to contact Storehouse were unsuccessful. "You see any of the others?"

"Taylor's hit. She's tying off a leg wound in the NW corner. She's a sitting duck unless we can get her out of there."

"We lost Davidson," he said, nodding to his right.

She looked, taking in, as he had, the unnatural angle the man's body had fallen, twisted and broken and devoid of life. He watched her blanch. "I say we fall back."

He stared into her beautiful face, smeared with camo paint. "Yeah. You're right."

He had no intention of falling back. He did, however, want her to get the hell out of there.

"Liar," she said.

He couldn't help his smile.

"So what's the plan...?"

MAX'S BLOOD RUSHED past her ears, her adrenaline running at levels she hadn't experienced in years, not since leaving Afghanistan, where she'd been stationed after Iraq, two years ago.

Three of their original team members found their way to them and radio contact with Lenny was finally established. Jackson filled him in on the situation. Max listened intently for his response, which, for all intents, should be to order them to fall back.

"Push on, Savage," was the order, instead.

Max's trigger finger itched with the desire to shoot someone other than hostiles.

What was she talking about? Lenny was a hostile.

They'd already pow-wowed with the four remaining uninjured members, got Taylor over the wall and to safety, and then decided they were all in. Now they had to rework the original strategy and get those hostages out.

Within minutes, they each had their plans and

split up, aware that around every corner lay the potential of running into guards.

"Wait!" she called, catching sight of something.

Everyone double-timed back.

"There," she said, pointing to the northeast guesthouse some hundred yards to their right.

It had seemed strange to her that a counterattack hadn't been made against them. Now she understood why: the compound guards had been moved to protect that guesthouse.

Somewhere in the back of her mind, a time clock ticked down. There was little doubt calls had been made and reinforcements were even now on their way. They had maybe five minutes to do what needed to be done and get out of Dodge.

"Odds are good they're being held in there," Jackson agreed.

"Could be the warlord."

He shook his head. "No. A number of guards also went into the main house, which means there's someone there, as well."

She considered him for a long moment. "Should we split up? Hit both?"

He shook his head. "No. Too risky. This is a one shot deal." He looked at the others. "I say we make a run on the guesthouse."

The others immediately agreed.

Of course, deciding to go that route was more easily said than done. Of the three structures, it was the most difficult to reach. There was no cover. It was all open territory between here and there.

Which was another reason it was most likely that's where the hostages were being held.

"Okay, here's the plan..." Jackson said.

WHILE HERSHEY AND EVANS focused on taking out the visible guards, he, Max and Bachman advanced in an uneven pattern, keeping an eye out for snipers. Selznick stayed near the wall where they would make their escape, providing any needed cover. By the time they reached the front of the two-story structure, the three visible guards had been taken out, and a fourth slumped forward from his hidden position just inside the open doorway. That coup had been compliments of Max, who must have spotted him a moment before Jackson had.

He and Max flanked the open door, while Bachman went around the back, followed by Evans and Hershey who continued to provide cover fire as they joined them.

Jackson nodded and then rushed the door at the same time Max aimed her weapon inside to provide any needed cover. They switched off like that three additional times, verifying there were no others on the first floor. They both looked up the stairs...

Evans joined them inside, leaving Hershey and Bachman at the front and back entrance.

"Cover me," Max said.

She began climbing the stairs and Jackson and

Evans aimed their weapons farther up, following after she was five steps up. They reached the second landing to find it empty.

Damn...

"Check 'em!" Max ordered.

One by one they checked all the rooms to find them empty.

Nothing.

No guards.

No warlord.

No hostages.

They double-timed it back out just as a series of Jeeps roared out of an unconnected garage near the front of the compound, nowhere near any of the three structures they'd been given to check.

"Let's get out of here," Max said next to him.

He couldn't have agreed more.

Of course, that decision proved to be as complicated as any they'd made thus far. As the convoy no doubt holding the hostages sped out, another set of vehicles sped in.

Gunfire spit at the ground at their feet.

"To the back!" he shouted.

He led the group through the empty house to the rear door. The containment wall lay twenty yards behind it. If they could make it there, they could scale it and be out, ordering Selznick to follow from his position farther up the wall.

The sound of gunfire filled the air.

He ran, blindly aiming his M-16 and shooting back, aware of Max doing the same on the other side of him. Evans took a direct shot and fell face first to the ground. Max instantly stopped and crouched, spraying their advancing enemy even as she checked their fallen team member. Jackson was pretty sure the man had taken it to the vest and was satisfied he would be okay when he awkwardly got to his feet with Max's one-armed help. Jackson provided cover fire as the others boosted Evans up and over the wall, then each of them followed.

Gunfire spit up the side of the wall, spraying cement fragments at him as he finally went over.

He wasn't surprised to find the sound of approaching vehicles outside. Disappointed, but not surprised.

They rushed to Storehouse who looked out of sorts, an injured Taylor leaning against a nearby tree, armed and ready for combat.

"Plan," Jackson demanded.

"Where are the hostages?"

"Gone."

"Bullshit! Get back in there and get them!"

"They're not there to get."

The roar of engines warned of imminent danger. "Plan?"

Lenny looked confused, and Jackson clearly saw panic settling in.

He grabbed the satellite communication device. "Who do I radio for backup?"

Lenny stared at him, half pissed, half scared. "Nobody. There is no backup. The SEAL team due to rendezvous with us was delayed."

"Exit point," Jackson said between clenched teeth.

"What do you mean there is no backup?" Polson, one of the other three of Storehouse's team that had made it out, but not without injury as the blood spreading on his upper thigh revealed, demanded. "Oh, fuck. We're gonna die, man. We're gonna die..."

Jackson shoved him toward the thick forest. "Not on my watch we're not..."

11

MAX HAD NO IDEA how they'd gotten away from the compound without further casualties. It had been part skill, part knowing how to utilize their surroundings, not to mention a massive infusion of luck, but a half an hour later there was nothing but the hushed sound of the team's uneven, labored breathing in the pre-dawn light, the rainforest around them beginning to come to life.

"Clear?" she said quietly.

Jackson looked down at her. "Clear."

Polson trudged over and sat down heavily on a tree stump. "Thank God…."

At some point in their retreat, Polson had regained his bearings and stood on his own two feet, feet that were now giving out. He collapsed to the ground and rested his head against his raised knees. Even Evans, who was by far more seriously injured, was holding up better than her male counterpart. A slight wince as she leaned against a nearby tree was the only giveaway that she was in pain.

Even though it had been a good fifteen minutes since they'd last heard anything from their pursuers, it would still be a good idea to keep their breather brief and trudge ahead.

She glanced over at where Jackson spoke to Polson. She noticed a ways back the right side of Jackson's face and right arm were red with blood. His own? Or someone else's?

Minutes later, he came over to find her going through her bag.

"What's the plan?" she asked.

"Exit near same place as entrance 1200 hours. We're going make camp here."

"Is that a good idea?"

"Is it a good idea to leave the same way we came?"

Before she realized she was going to do it, she was touching the side of his face. His eyes widened slightly and she quickly withdrew her hand.

"It's yours, the blood…"

He touched his fingers to it and then grimaced. "Spray from the wall, maybe."

How close he'd had to be to have the gunfire spit wall fragments hard enough to break his skin.

He nodded to his right. "There's a stream over there. Why don't you go and get cleaned up while I make camp?"

She gave him an amused smile. "Actually, I was

just going to suggest the same thing to you." She turned him in that direction. "Go on, I'll help set up camp."

He looked doubtful.

"Don't make me give you a square kick," she threatened.

He chuckled and moved away with a couple of the other guys toward the stream.

Max stood for long moment, watching after him. She didn't care what the others thought or didn't think. She was just glad that he was okay, that she was okay and that this entire mess was soon going to be behind them so they could...

The chaos of the past few hours made the idea of normal day-to-day life seem far away. But not so far that she couldn't grasp tightly onto it, hoping...

For what?

Oh, she knew.

Not that she was prepared to admit that to anyone. Not even herself.

But still that hope remained...

AN HOUR LATER, Jackson snuck into Max's tent. He was highly amused at her surprised expression. Dawn was just breaking, but down in the forest it was still dim, no backlight to illuminate what they might be doing inside. Two men were placed on perimeter duty and everyone but the leader was down for a rest before making the final hike to the rendezvous point.

"Hey," he said, crouching and taking in where she was still fully dressed. "Aren't you going to get out of those?"

She arched a brow at him. He'd watched as she washed up in the stream, pouring water over her curly hair, scrubbing her face neck and arms. She looked as fresh as if she'd taken a long, hot shower.

"And wear what?" she asked quietly.

He plucked a small Baggie of cookies off her bedroll. "Oh, I don't know. Nothing?" He held up the sweets.

"Compliments of my mother. She must have shoved them in my pack when I wasn't looking. Go ahead."

He fished one of the cookies out. It had to be the best thing he tasted—outside Max—in years.

Of course, he knew his reaction had to do with their close call. Heightened senses were common following such an incredible adrenaline rush.

"What else did she put in there?" he asked, reaching for her bag.

She snatched it out of reach. "None of your business."

He finished the cookie. "You know, it's not good to have stuff like that in the wild."

"Tell my mother."

He grinned. "I will."

"Good luck with that."

She smiled and something flipped over inside of him.

Whoa.

It seemed his sense of taste wasn't the only thing heightened in the wake of their recent gun battle.

Merely looking at her made him hotter than he could ever remember being.

Despite what had already passed between them, he tried telling himself this was Max, his friend, and now his coworker. He needed to keep that fact straight.

There was no mixing business with pleasure...

Or sex with friendship...

"Wh...what are you doing?" she whispered.

He hadn't realized he'd leaned in toward her until their breath mingled in the short space between them.

"This..."

He kissed her.

She appeared ready to deny him. He slid his lips against hers one way, then the other...and then claimed them full on.

Her soft sigh fluttered like butterfly wings against his face and she relaxed into him, her hands pulling him to her. The feel of her breasts against his chest ignited an even hotter fire deep in his groin. He leaned farther in and zipped the tent door before tipping her to lie flat against her bedding.

So much for good intentions.

Sweet Lord, she was sexy...

He nudged her knees apart with his and filled the space between them, pressing his hardness against her softness. He ran his hand up her narrow waist to cup her breast, his thumb finding her nipple through the fabric of her tank and bra. She made a quiet sound somewhere between a moan and a whimper and pressed her hips up into his.

He groaned in the back of his throat then chuckled.

"What?" she whispered, kissing the side of his mouth.

"Nothing. It's just that…" He stared into her half-lidded eyes. "This is the first time I've kissed a fellow Marine."

She smiled and moved her hands to his backside, pressing him even harder against her. "Well, I certainly hope kissing isn't the only thing you're planning on doing…"

He rubbed the side of his face against hers and pressed his lips against her earlobe. "Depends…"

She gasped when he lightly pinched her nipple. "On what?"

"Hmm?" he asked, gazing down at her.

"You said it depends. Depends on what?"

He kissed her neck. "Oh, I don't know. Maybe on whether or not you can keep quiet. Because the other night, you scared the cat…"

Her squeak of laughter inspired his own. "I did not!"

"You did so…"

He grinned and kissed her until she sighed back

into the bedding, her breathing ragged, her body trembling. Then he allowed his right hand to roam.

Tugging the hem of her tank from her khakis, he slid his fingers underneath, splaying them against her stomach. He worked his thumb under the edge of her bra cup, rasping it over a stiff nipple. His mouth watered with the desire to taste her, to pull the puckered flesh into his mouth, feel the texture of her against his tongue. But this was neither the time nor the place for leisurely desire. And even if he couldn't keep his hands to himself, he had to keep in mind where they were and what might happen at any moment.

He slid his hand back down her abdomen. She sucked in her breath and he used the advantage to budge his fingers inside the front of her pants, not stopping until the tips were under the elastic of her panties. She was so wet, so hot...

And his erection grew so hard it was nearly painful. He removed his hand and undid the front of her pants, allowing him more comfortable access. She began to shimmy out of them, but he held her fast.

"No, leave them on."

She stared at him, her mouth half open in question, until he slid his hand back inside to rest between her thighs.

She opened herself to him farther and he stifled a groan, yearning to stroke her with more than his fingers.

He parted her with his thumb and index finger,

then ran his middle along the length of her slick channel, up to her button and back down again. Her back came up off the ground, pressing her sex hard against the heel of his hand. He dipped his middle finger inside her, pulled it out and then slid it in to the hilt. She moaned low and sweet. Finding her clit, he rubbed it lightly with his index finger even as he thrust his thumb deep inside her.

Her reaction was nothing short of mesmerizing. He watched her breasts heave, her mouth suck in air as if she couldn't get enough of it, and her hips move as she hotly ground against him…

It took every ounce of self-restraint he had not to strip her down and replace his thumb with his throbbing cock. He wanted her so badly he could taste her orgasm in the back of his throat.

He leaned in and kissed her, claiming her open mouth. She hungrily returned the attention, one of her hands curving around the back of his head, the other winding around his right wrist as if caught between wanting to pull him away, and wanting to keep him there.

"Please…" she whimpered, pleading with her eyes as well as her words. "I want to feel you…"

"Shhhh, I want to feel you, too, baby," he whispered back, then trapped whatever she might have added with his mouth against hers.

He stimulated her clit with his fingers, drawing tight, wet circles even as he twisted his thumb, applying pressure to the back of her vagina then the front, curving it against her G-spot...

Her muscles contracted almost instantly and her back came up off the floor. He swallowed her moan and kissed her hard in an attempt to stifle her sounds, as well as to keep himself from pulling her pants down and entering her, if just for a sweet, torturous minute.

Finally, she collapsed against the bedroll, spent, her eyes liquid jade as she gazed at him. His back teeth hurt from the effort it took not to claim her fully.

She reached out, trapping his hard-on between his stomach and her hand.

Jackson pulled her to him until he spooned her. She made sounds of approval and wriggled her sweet bottom against him. He groaned.

"Hold still."

"No."

He closed his eyes and took a deep breath. Damn, but the woman was going to be the death of him.

As he counted backward from a thousand, a small voice in the back of his head told him it would be a hell of a way to go...

12

MAX WOKE TO FIND herself alone. She snuggled deeper into the bedroll, wishing Jax was still curved against her. The sun shone more brightly through the ceiling of tree branches, turning the top of her tent into a kaleidoscope of shifting light.

Was it even possible she'd escaped this godawful hellhole for a short, precious time? Yet somehow he had made it happen for her. He'd selflessly stroked away her tension and fear, made her forget who she was, where she was and inspired her to feel nothing but joy.

Feel nothing but him…

She could have easily been lying under the old oak tree behind her aunt's farmhouse on a picnic blanket on a warm summer's day…

She smiled into her arm where she rested her face against it.

Jax…

How many times had she lain under that tree back home and daydreamed about him? Lived a fantasy life full of picnics and bike rides and make-out sessions in the cab of his truck?

Of course, they'd never done any of that. She'd been far too stubborn, and he had been far too busy.

But now...

She rolled over to lie on her back, smiling at the low tent top. How beautiful he'd been, back then and now. There were a few times when she'd almost told him, almost kissed him when it seemed she had no control over her actions. But something had always interfered. More than a few times, it had been another girl...

She rubbed her closed eyes, wanting to wash away the image of Jax with another woman, oust the pain that accompanied it.

Blondes. They'd almost always been blondes. Petite perky ones that smiled a lot and appeared ready to burst into a cheer at any moment. She'd hated them all on sight. She realized now her urge to knock the smiles off their faces hadn't had anything to do with their hair color, but rather because they'd been the focus of Jackson's attention.

The only saving grace was, they'd never lasted long.

She wondered about that now. Why hadn't they? In fact, she couldn't seem to recall him dating any single female for longer than maybe a month.

She'd been so obsessed with her own reaction, she'd never stopped to ponder his motivations.

And if a time or two she had considered dying her hair blond, well, that was between her and the supermarket cashier...

She stared at where she twirled one of the red curls that had escaped her ponytail around her finger. Usually, she'd stop such girly, self-indulgent behavior whenever she caught it. But not now.

Now she allowed herself the harmless indulgence, if only because she was enjoying it.

Enjoying the feeling of being in love.

Her throat grew tight as she realized that's what had taken hold of her. Not that she had anything to compare it to. She'd certainly never visited this territory before. Never ventured beyond the haze of physical attraction to what might lie beyond.

She'd never been tempted to.

Then again, it really wasn't a temptation, was it? It either happened or it didn't.

She now understood something her mother had said, something she'd once judged as moronic: "Oh, when you're in love, you'll know it."

She smiled. Yeah, she was very definitely in love...

The unmistakable sound of gunfire shredded the calm silence and rent her meanderings in two.

Max grabbed her M-16 and dived for the tent

door, watching as holes ripped through the wall and into the bedding she'd been on a moment before.

Her heart thundered in her chest for reasons unrelated to ones just a moment before. Her head swam from the short distance between the two extremes, pure adrenaline flooding her bloodstream.

Get it together, get it together....

It boggled her mind that moments before, she'd been thanking Jax for the escape....

Now she wondered if she should have been cursing him....

She scrambled out and across the clearing for cover in the trees, her breath coming in shallow gasps. What was going on? Had their pursuers followed them that far into the forest?

She glanced at her watch. Only twenty minutes before they were due to make the final hike to the rendezvous point.

Timing was everything when it came to assignments of this nature. One minute earlier, one minute later and everything was thrown off.

And twenty minutes later they would have been long gone. Whoever was now targeting the camp would have found nothing but footprints and the Baggie that held her mother's cookies.

A split second earlier and she would have been lying where those bullets had hit...

She watched as Polson rushed from his tent, hitting the tree next to her. A few others followed, mostly her fellow team members, flanking other trees nearby.

Where was Jackson?

Leading with her gun, she scanned the now silent area, nothing but a few falling leaves and bird screeches indicating anything had happened.

Nothing. Not a hint of friend or foe.

She reached for her radio.

Jackson immediately responded.

Thank God.

He indicated he was on the northern perimeter and would be coming in. She was to sit tight until then.

Well, she certainly wasn't about to sit loose.

"Where's Lenny?" she asked Polson.

"Haven't seen him."

She took in the three remaining tents. All of them bore the same holes hers did. Had the other team members been sleeping at the time of the attack? Were they even now inside, dead?

She needed to check. Lenny was in the first tent, if she wasn't mistaken.

"Cover me," she said to Polson.

"From who?"

She grabbed his gun and pointed it around the tree. "From anyone who shoots at me."

Taking a deep breath, she swung around and made a beeline for the tent. Nothing. She wasn't sure if that was good or bad. She decided since she was still alive, it was good.

She pushed open the tent flap with her gun. Lying inside was Lenny. He was dead.

Damn.

She reached for his satellite phone, only to snatch her hand back when gunfire sounded and more bullets ripped up the side of the tent.

Shit!

She backtracked toward her tree, relieved when Polson provided cover fire.

"So?" he asked.

"Dead."

"Shit."

"My thoughts exactly."

Given there was still no movement from the other tents, she assumed that only Polson had made it out alive from the other team. Which made her doubly grateful that their team was full and accounted for.

There was still no way of telling who was targeting them, or how many of them there were. Although it was safe to say they were on the other side of the camp. Had they been on this side, well, that body count might very well be the other way around.

"Where are you going?" Polson whispered harshly.

"To see who our friends are."

"Savage said to sit tight."

She stared at him. "Right. And that's exactly

what you and the others are going to do. Sit tight and cover me..."

She darted for the next tree, Polson's profanity following her. She stared at him and indicated he should be looking out for her. He cursed some more then swung to do as she requested.

She made it to the third tree before she took hostile fire. It didn't help that it was a young tree, not only not providing much cover, but narrow enough rounds might make it through.

She hunched down low to the ground and darted for the next tree, pausing against it and closing her eyes as she took fire again.

She couldn't be sure how close she was, but she figured it was close enough if they were firing at her. Only she wasn't convinced it was a 'they' but rather was one person. Two at most.

Of course, he or they currently held the advantage—they were in a stationary position while she was on the move.

She moved again.

Unfortunately, it appeared her adversary was, too, given the angle of fire.

She lifted her radio. "Polson, keep a watch to your right."

"Why?"

"Target heading your way."

She heard him curse without the radio.

All she could do was hope he stayed put and

didn't drop back. Last thing she needed was to worry about her team.

Of course, she wasn't all that keen on running around in circles, either.

Following the next move, she crouched down and angled her weapon around the tree trunk, scanning the opposite side with her scope.

There!

Problem was, her adversary was aiming his weapon directly back at her.

She squeezed off a shot and then ducked for cover.

She swallowed hard. That was too close for comfort.

She estimated the distance between Polson and the shooter. Four trees. Polson should be able to see him by now.

Then why hadn't he taken a shot?

She picked up the radio.

No answer.

Shit!

She tried to make him out, but could see nothing.

Great. Either he had bought it, or had fallen back. Either way, that meant she was on her own.

She backtracked a tree, sweat trickling down the back of her neck. She waited a heartbeat, and then slowly aimed her weapon around the trunk.

Again, she found herself scope to scope with her opponent.

She was about to pull the trigger when the barrel of his was weapon lifted up.

Max looked with her bare eye, then through the scope again, adjusting the distance for a broader view.

Someone stood to the shooter's left, holding a handgun to the man's temple.

Jackson...

Her relief was so complete she nearly dissolved into a puddle.

"All clear," Polson called.

She lifted herself to a standing position, her back against the tree, not for cover, but to support her liquefied knees. She edged around, still holding her weapon at the ready. Jackson walked out the gunman, while Polson walked another one out from another direction.

She smiled at them both. "Well, hello, boys. Imagine running into you here."

Jackson directed Polson to detain his captive while he did the same. Max provided backup as they updated each other...

It appeared they were the last three left out of the crew that had stayed behind.

Damn.

"Sat com is dead," Max said, referring to the satellite phone.

"Damn." Jackson had whispered the word but it held the impact of a shout.

"What do we do now?"

"Move to the rendezvous point and hope we're still getting picked up."

Max glanced at her watch, thinking they were already behind, only to find only twenty minutes had passed and they were right on target for the hike to the clearing.

It was all about timing.

The moment the thought entered her mind, she was being grabbed from behind and gunfire deafened her.

13

JACKSON DIVED FOR POLSON, knocking him down to the dirt and falling on top of him. The two captives jerked like marionettes in a sick puppet show then crumpled in lifeless heaps mere feet away.

Even with everything going on, all he could think of was Max...

He rolled away and aimed his weapon, catching the man holding her captive in his sights.

Damn!

Too close.

He wiped at the instant sweat that coated his brow and squinted again. The guy was good. Too good. He knew how to hold Max in front of him as a shield. While Jackson was a crack shot, he couldn't trust himself. Not with emotion surging as well as adrenaline.

Not recognizing the fear that threatened to paralyze him.

He glanced to find Polson lifting his weapon. He smacked it so the round bit the ground a few feet away. His own team members were off to the left and were waiting on his lead.

The chances of hitting her were too great.

Max was pulled from view behind the trees.

Damn it!

Jackson scrambled to his feet only to find himself targeted by more gunfire.

He and Polson rushed for cover.

But he didn't stay there. He *couldn't* stay there.

Without a second thought, he ran to his left, skirting around the trees, his legs pumping, his heart hammering, his palms damp against his M-16. He came up on one of the first startled gunmen fast, taking him out before the guy could even blink, and kept running, not stopping until he was on the guy holding Max.

He hesitated. Or it felt as if he did. In reality, he hadn't stopped moving. He recognized the slow motion of his thoughts. The stop-motion animation. His adrenaline-flooded brain registered everything in sharp photo quality, allowing him to note details he might not have otherwise seen. It was the same sensation that allowed for lifesaving knee-jerk reactions when you were in danger.

It was that same hyperconsciousness that allowed him to register within a glance, the way the captor held Max, the angle of the gun he pressed against her temple, the fact that his attention was focused ahead of him and not on Jackson.

He launched himself against the gunman hard, the stop-motion animation vanishing and returning to real time the instant Jackson's flesh crashed against the flesh of his opponent in a bone-jarring smack.

They both fell to the ground along with Max.

Before they hit the dirt, twenty thoughts ricocheted through his head, the top of them being how stupid he was. He had no idea if there was another gunman or several, or if the pistol the captor had held against Max's temple had a hair trigger, no matter the angle he'd held it.

But he was running on pure adrenaline, his only aim to free Max as soon as he could, pre-planning and caution be damned.

He didn't realize he was pummeling the guy until he saw the barrel of an M-16 in front of him, pointed at the gunman's head.

He blinked up to find Max smiling at him. "Got it."

The hostile wasn't the only one she'd gotten. She had him as well....

The thought filled the void left by the fleeing urgency, large and loud and undeniable.

And it concerned him nearly as much as the idea of her being harmed.

Yes, Max had him. Lock, stock and two smoking barrels.

Somewhere down the line, their friendship had evolved into a hot affair then rushed toward something much more.

The question was, what was he going to do about it?

The answer that immediately came to him was the same as his response about what to do with the situation at hand—he intended to escape as quickly as he could...

MAX COULDN'T PINPOINT exactly what, but within the squeeze of a trigger, something had changed. Jackson, well, he was behaving oddly. Not like the Jax she knew, either as a friend, or a lover.

Directly after he'd climbed off her captor, he'd stalked away as if upset; with himself or her, she couldn't be sure. And when he came back after checking the area, he seemed to pointedly keep his distance, avoiding her gaze and leaving her questions—even simple ones—unanswered.

Jackson, Max and what was left of the team hiked toward the rendezvous point with Jax in the lead. He appeared to be sweating more than she had ever seen him do before, his handsome face set in deep, somber lines.

Her heart still beat heavily from her brief hostage stint. She'd never had control taken from her in that way before, but training had served her well. She'd been reviewing her escape options and had felt confident of success when Jackson had appeared from out of nowhere and taken the guy down.

They reached the clearing and stopped, Polson propping his hands against his knees. "Where they at?"

Max looked at Jackson who looked at the sky. A chopper was supposed to come in and pluck them out, then take them to a nearby landing strip where a plane was waiting.

Only there was no chopper.

Was Lenny to have radioed first?

If so, they were out of luck. The radio had been shot along with Lenny.

"We wait," he said stonily.

"For how long?" Polson demanded.

Jackson stared at him, then turned away. Max felt his distance as cold as any December wind now blowing back home.

"Shut up, Polson," Taylor said, earning agreement from the other four team members where they hung around on the perimeter, keeping an eye out even as they focused on their leader.

They couldn't stay long. Not now that it was obvious they were being pursued. It was important they get out of the area as quickly as possible.

"We'll wait fifteen," Jackson said.

"And then?" Max asked.

He didn't say anything. Instead he shrugged off

his sack, placed it on a nearby rock and went to the side of the river where he splashed water over his handsome face.

She wanted to stalk after him, demand to know what was going on.

Instead, she let her own sack slide to the ground where she sat on it, watching as Polson and a few of the others did the same.

Fifteen minutes came and went with each of them searching the sky, while keeping a furtive eye on the surrounding jungle.

Nothing.

Polson pushed from his sack and paced. "They're not coming." He issued a staccato litany of profanity. "I'm beginning to think we were never meant to get out of here alive."

"Don't be stupid," Jackson said. "What purpose would our deaths serve?"

"Once they knew the mission was unsuccessful?" Polson asked. "I don't now? To save a buck and cut risk?"

Max rubbed her forehead. Even in the military sometimes decisions were made not to retrieve if the target area was too hot. But never to save a dollar.

Could Polson be right? Were they expendable? Just another entry on a spreadsheet?

Jackson finally glanced at her, the shadow in his eyes unreadable. She steadily returned his gaze. Then he walked to his sack, bent and opened a side pocket, sliding out what looked like little more than a glorified cellular phone. But she knew it was a satellite phone.

Relief flushed through her, complete and overwhelming.

Polson let loose an excited shout that sent birds fleeing from neighboring trees.

Selznick hit him in the arm...hard.

"What? Oh. Sorry." He ran his hand over his close-cropped hair and back again, grinning. "It's just I feel like a deathrow inmate who's just been granted a reprieve."

Jackson frowned at him. "Yeah, well, don't get too excited. I don't know if I'm going to be able to do anything to get us out of here."

"Hell, give me the phone and I'll call my sister," Polson said. "She'll fly over and rent a car to drive in if she has to."

Jackson ignored him and turned to walk away.

Max had no fear. She knew Jackson would get them out, even if they had to hike to the next village and buy their way out.

What concerned her more than their current predicament was what was going through his head.

That frightened her more than being taken hostage again. Because while she knew how to survive a hostile situation, she wasn't so sure she knew how to survive if he turned away from her.

LOOKING INTO MAX's pain-filled and questioning eyes was too difficult, so he made a point of not doing it.

Jackson placed the call directly to Lincoln Williams rather than through Lazarus Security for two reasons: one, he knew Linc would ask him no questions and would put his government connections to quick use and two, he'd prefer his brother Jason not know about this.

Five minutes later, he broke the connection and stood staring at the quiet forest. Linc had promised to get back to him within minutes with exit details.

"Jax?"

The quiet question in Max's voice touched a spot so deep inside him, he was afraid he might never close it off again. He looked at her before realizing he shouldn't have, taking the moment to drink in her face.

Even all smudged and dirty, with remnants of camo paint, she was still the most beautiful woman he'd ever known. Oh, maybe not strictly physically, but that wasn't the point. What he knew of her inside, the way her mind worked, the way her heart worked, it all combined to make her the most beautiful person he'd ever been lucky enough to cross paths with.

And it was because of that, he couldn't allow this, whatever was happening between them, to go any further. He'd only hurt her. And he couldn't bear that.

Only the idea of stopping what had already started, was hurting him. Go figure.

An immediately recognizable light of hope sparked in her green eyes.

He forced himself to look away.

The satellite phone rang. He turned and answered it, pacing some ways away first.

"Got it," Linc said.

Two minutes later he had a plan. It wasn't an ideal one. But it would get them all out of there alive and in one piece.

Which was more than anyone had expected a half hour ago.

Pointedly ignoring Max, he slid the phone into his sack and then hoisted it onto his shoulders.

"We're out of here. Let's go...."

14

MAX'S BONES SAGGED as she exited the military transport plane and descended the stairs to the Colorado Springs tarmac. The December wind blew hard, freezing her teeth, reminding her Christmas was next week…and that the cold outside had nothing to do with the cold that gripped her from within.

They'd left with sixteen and returned with eight. Polson was the only surviving member from the other team.

The reality ripped straight through her.

She'd confronted some pretty hairy situations during her six-year stint in the service, but nothing that resulted in such a high mortality rate. While still in the thick of things, you learned to push such realities aside, adrenaline helping keep you focused.

But now that she was home and reality was more about Christmas carols and colored lights, the contrast made her dizzy.

As did Jackson's odd behavior.

She watched him as he shook hands and shared a hug with a tall, dark man near the arrivals building. Was he the one responsible for helping with their exit? She'd chance a yes. While she'd like nothing better than to express her appreciation for the man's assistance, right now she didn't think she could handle any more icy treatment from Jackson for fear she might shatter.

She guessed it went without saying she was grateful....

Back in the clearing in that godforsaken, hostile-filled jungle, Polson had balked at the thought of more hiking when Jackson had issued a curt, "Let's go." Max reminded Polson that even if they had to make wings out of feathers they found on the ground and fly out of there, they would do what it took.

Of course, she'd had no idea at the time that the journey ahead of them would be as long as the journey behind them. They'd trekked fifteen klicks toward the coast, one of the most dangerous hot spots for warlord activities, ditching their sacks and all but the most basic of their weaponry outside town before going in to rendezvous with their contact. Polson had nearly shit himself when they'd approached a group of well-armed men who looked much like the hostiles they'd already encountered. In fact, Max wouldn't be surprised if they'd been connected to the same gang.

It was the largest of the men Jackson had spoken to. And within moments, all eight of them were being led to a large compound within the city.

Polson hadn't wanted to enter. Max had to admit she was a little leery about subjecting herself to further scrutiny, especially since the all-male army appeared very interested in her and Taylor.

But she trusted Jackson. And after meeting with what appeared to be one of the high commanders, they were driven to the coast where they caught a boat transport to meet up with another, captained by people Jackson appeared to know.

Within twenty-four hours, they were safe and stateside.

Strangely, Max wouldn't have minded being still trapped in that jungle together, hostiles and all, so long as it meant Jackson would look at her again.... Touch her....

"Maxine!"

She was startled to hear her name called the instant she walked inside the arrivals hub. She had to blink three times to make sure she wasn't seeing things as her mother rushed up to hug her.

The extreme shift of emotion caught her off guard. She dropped her gear and hugged her mother back in a way she couldn't remember doing since she was a kid, allowing herself an unguarded moment of indulgence. She closed her eyes, breathing in the scent of Tabu, her mother's perfume, and absorbing her softness.

"Oh, honey, are you okay?" her mother murmured, but didn't try to move away. "What happened?"

Max opened her eyes to catch Jackson looking at her, the expression on his face warming her...and confusing her.

She'd had no idea he'd called her mother to meet her there. She was grateful. And heartbroken. She hadn't known what she'd expected, hoped? That he might take her home? That she might finally get a chance to talk to him? Ask him what was going through his head?

Now she wasn't going to get that.

And what about him? Who would be looking after him?

Her mother finally drew back just a bit and smoothed her hair back from her face. "You look like you've been through hell and back."

Funny, she felt as if she had. In more ways than one.

She looked around as the remaining team members greeted their families. It appeared her mother wasn't the only one Jax had contacted.

"Come on. I know you don't like to talk about stuff. So let's just get you home and into a nice, hot bath." She linked arms with her. "And maybe later we can go Christmas shopping."

Max found comfort in her mother's ramblings as they headed toward the exit, but not enough to touch the pool of pain growing in her chest. She looked over her shoulder at Jackson, but found he had turned to continue talking to the man he'd met outside. While she walked forward, she felt oddly like her feet were stuck in mud, time having stopped at the moment she'd looked into his eyes and registered everything had changed.

And she had no idea how to go about starting it up again...

"HEY, MAN," LINCOLN Williams said. "You okay?"

Jackson hauled his gaze away from Max's retreating back, although his thoughts remained with her. He was glad her mother made it in to pick her up. He hadn't told Cindy much beyond the fact that Max had been through a difficult mission and would need a ride home. But just knowing she was going to be looked after made him feel better.

But not as good as he'd hoped it would.

"Yeah. I'm fine. Thanks to you."

He considered the man who had not hesitated to do the impossible by getting him and the others out of Africa. Linc had served with his brother Jason and was one of the partners at Lazarus Security. A fellow ex-Marine, then F.B.I., none of them were sure of the extent of his connections. They just knew they were considerable.

As recent events merely served to prove.

"No problem. I'd have been upset if you hadn't called me."

"Chances are I'd be dead if I hadn't called you."

"No. I'm sure you would have gotten you and your remaining team members out."

Polson came up, effusively thanked Linc, grudgingly acknowledged Jackson, then told him he'd meet up with him back at Pegasus the following day.

"Sorry, man, but I won't be going back," Jackson said, shaking his hand.

"What? Scared?"

Jackson chuckled without humor. "Yeah. Of their piss-poor support. I'd advise you to look elsewhere, as well."

He knew some tended to forget the heat of battle the instant they were out of it. Polson appeared to be one of them. He'd rush right back into the fray, having forgotten everything that had come before. The word "lesson" was completely foreign to him.

While it bothered Jackson to think the guy would be going back to that piece of shit operation, it was Polson's decision. And this was where his responsibilities officially ended.

As for his team, he'd spoken to them on the plane and not one was going back.

"Yeah, right," Polson said, grinning. "See you around then."

"Yeah. Good luck."

Polson walked away, chuckling.

"I don't know him and already I don't like him," Linc said.

Jackson nodded. "Yeah. Real ass."

"Maybe you should have left him back in the jungle."

Jackson looked at him. "I'm just glad someone else outside my team made it out alive."

Linc's eyes narrowed. He didn't know the entire story. And Jackson wasn't up to telling him just then...if ever.

"Who's the girl?"

He frowned.

"Don't play that. I saw the way you were looking at her."

Jackson laughed. He'd heard it rumored that the once silent Linc had gone all soft lately. He understood it was because he'd fallen for some girl who now lived in Maine and was the reason Linc worked the majority of the time out of Boston now. But he wouldn't have believed it unless he'd seen it.

He shrugged. "Just some girl I went to school with...."

He winced even as he said the words.

He'd never referred to Max in such an indifferent way. She'd always been the girl next door, his best friend.

Now?

He stretched his neck and set his jaw.

"Yeah. Just some girl," Linc agreed with disagreement. He put an arm over his shoulders. "Come on, let's get out of here. You're stinking up the place in more ways than one."

Jackson picked up his sack and they walked out. If he was hoping Max and her mom were still somewhere nearby, he wasn't admitting to it, even to himself.

Linc led him to a black Mercedes with tinted windows. It belonged to the Lazarus fleet, he knew. Bullet-proof and tweaked for double the performance of the regular model.

"By the way," Linc said as he popped the trunk. "I talked to your brother earlier."

Jackson's movements slowed as he hoisted his gear inside. "Did you say anything?"

Linc closed the trunk. "Of course not."

His friend stood looking at him for a long moment.

"But you think I should," Jackson finally said.

"You've got to do what you think best. But, yeah, I do think you need to tell him."

The mere idea of him telling his older brother he had gone off on that dumbass mission, much less that he'd failed at it and had relied on Linc to get him out made Jackson's teeth ache.

"He and Jordan are coming in for the holidays tomorrow."

The holidays.

God, he'd completely forgotten. He'd been so preoccupied, he'd barely noticed it wasn't ninety degrees with a hundred percent humidity.

He blinked and looked around. Everyone seemed to be greeting family members just arriving and "Jingle Bells" was piped through the airport's sound system.

He grimaced.

"Come on. I'll take you out to your grandmother's place."

Jackson shook his head as they headed for opposite doors. "My truck's at Pegasus. I'd much rather you took me there."

"Then you'll head to your grandmother's?"

No, he planned to go to his apartment in town. Cleo would be missing him. Chuck had been looking after her while he was gone, but it wasn't the same.

"Since when have you become a mother hen?"

Linc threw his head back and laughed harder than Jackson had ever seen him do. Then they both got into the car…

15

MAX FELT JUST this side of roadkill.

She cracked her eyes open to find dreary daylight filling her room. She sighed and rolled onto her back, her arm across her eyes. She'd been back a day, and had slept most of it, but yearned for more. A full week at least.

She peered at the clock and then covered her eyes again. It was just after nine. She was surprised neither her mom nor aunt had come in after her yet. They'd hovered over her so much yesterday, she'd been forced to ask them for some privacy.

They'd looked so hurt, she'd winced at her abrasiveness.

Truth was, she'd never spoken to either of them about some of the horrors she'd seen during her tour in the military. And she never would. It almost seemed like some sort of unwritten rule among the

Marines. Forget Vegas. What happened on the battlefield, stayed on the battlefield.

Oh, counselors encouraged them to speak. Communication was comparable to disarming an emotional land mine, one of them had once told her. But how did she explain to her mother and aunt what she'd seen? Wasn't it bad enough she had nightmares that kept her up at night? Did she really want to plant the images in their minds so they could keep her company?

No. Better they not know the details.

Especially about this latest mission.

Images screamed through her head, one after the other, the rapid report of gunfire deafening her.

She drew in a deep breath and let it out. While the experiences of the past few days were indirectly to blame for her revisiting old memories, she knew she was distracting herself from the truth of her deep sense of melancholy: Jackson Savage.

She glanced toward the window. She couldn't count the times she'd padded across the room to stare out onto the frozen landscape, wondering if he'd come out to his grandmother's home or stayed in town. She'd held her cell phone tightly in both hands, longing to call him. She'd even dialed once and quickly hung up, praying her number hadn't had a chance to register on his end, yet not caring if it had.

What hurt beyond all else was that she had no

clue what had happened. No idea what had made him turn from her so completely. If she knew, she could formulate a plan to deal with it, dress her wound and limp on. Instead she felt as if she was bleeding to death.

There was a soft rap at the door.

Max squeezed her eyes closed tighter.

"Maxi?" The hinges squeaked as her mom ventured inside the room. "You awake?"

"Yeah," she said softly.

Moments later the mattress shifted slightly. Max opened her eyes to see her mother sitting down beside her. Concern was etched so deeply on her face, it made Max hurt.

"How are you feeling this morning?"

Tears stung the back of her eyes, surprising her.

"Oh, honey…" Cindy moved in and gathered Max in her arms, something she hadn't done since Max was a young girl. "Shhh…it'll be okay. Everything'll be okay. You just wait and see."

Max tried to find the strength to fight, but instead surrendered, weeping nakedly against her mother's shoulder…

JACKSON HAD A LIST the length of his forearm to complete, yet all he could do was sit at his kitchen table staring at his cup full of cold coffee.

He was exhausted yet he hadn't slept a wink. He was hungry, but couldn't bring himself to eat. He was hurting, but couldn't seem to do anything to address the pain.

So he merely sat.

Cleo leaped onto the table and padded over to him, rubbing her nose against the side of his face. He blinked, registering that her nose was cold, and she was purring, but unable to do much more.

He didn't get it. He'd seen dozens of battles. Had witnessed countless casualties. Faced brutal opponents. Yet he couldn't ever remember a time when he'd felt this out of it before.

He distantly registered the ringing of his cell phone but couldn't remember where it was, much less answer it.

He began lifting his cup, then forgot why and put it back down.

Cleo stopped cleaning her flank long enough to stare at him, then walked over to the cup and stuck her nose inside. The sound of her lapping was loud in the otherwise silent apartment.

Jason...

He winced. His brother was going to freak when he found out Jackson had used Lazarus Security resources to get out of Africa.

Damn.

That was one conversation he wasn't looking forward to having. He could already hear Jason saying "I told you so" in several different languages and myriad tones of voice when it came to his warning against signing with Pegasus.

As for any future he might have had with Lazarus: gone.

That was probably for the best. If these past few days had proven anything to him, it was that his brother was right.

He snorted.

At least that part of the conversation Jason would enjoy.

"Hey, big brother, you were right. I'm not cut out for this business. You'll be happy to know I now get that I'm a complete, abject failure...."

The words wove around his brain and back, settling somewhere near his solar plexus. He absently rubbed his chest, imagining Jason's self-satisfied grin.

He closed his eyes, thinking of the men he'd lost in Africa. There was no taking that back. No erasing the visions of their dead and dying bodies. No chance at another shot to make things different.

He lifted his cup and took a sip of the cold coffee, grimacing when he had to take a long, black cat hair out of the side of his mouth. Cleo stared at him as if to say, "So?"

He pushed from the table, dumped the cup's contents into the sink, rinsed it, then took the vodka bottle out of the freezer and poured a finger inside the cup. He knocked it back, stood for a moment, then took the bottle out again. He carried both back to the table, pouring as he went.

Hey, at least he wasn't drinking straight from the bottle. And if he needed any more, he could always go downstairs to The Barracks to get it.

Cleo checked out the change in beverage then glared at him. He lifted a brow, then watched as she flicked her tail and leaped from the table.

Not even his cat wanted his company.

Fine.

The cell phone rang again. He ignored it.

So what did he do now? Did he go back to work downstairs? Take the path Jason had mapped out for him and expand the bar's food offerings? Become the cook everyone suggested he should be?

He downed the vodka and poured another.

Of course, he could always just sit here and pickle himself....

Yeah, just then, that option was the most appealing.

The fact that he wasn't much of a drinker became immediately apparent. Of course, his exhausted state might also be contributing to the lightheadedness he felt.

Max.

The name he'd banned from his head floated in on wings and stayed there.

Damn it all to hell and back. What had he been thinking when he'd allowed things to get personal between them? When he'd given himself over to feelings he had probably always harbored for her, but never acted on?

He grabbed the vodka so violently a portion spilled over the top of the bottle.

What was he talking about? He'd had as much say in what had happened between them as he did in the price of gas.

Was it really only a few nights ago he'd kissed her for the first time right over there in the living room? Tasted her lips? Felt the heaviness of her breasts in his hands? Slid his fingers down between her thighs to find her hot for him?

His back teeth were clenched so tightly together it took effort to loosen them so he could down another slug of vodka.

As expected, the memories that trailed those were what had gone down in Africa....

His sheer terror when they'd first taken gunfire, his only concern for her safety. Her being held captive. Her melting against his hand when he'd given into the urge to touch her when they'd lain together in the tent.

His cell phone again.

He awkwardly pushed from the table, staggering a little as he crossed to his bedroom. It took a few moments, but he finally located his cell in the pile he'd emptied out of his sack on his bed.

He answered without checking the display.

"What the fuck do you want?"

There was a heartbeat of silence, then, "You kiss your grandmother with that mouth?"

Jackson grimaced and collapsed to sit on top of the bed. Shit.

"Hey, Gram. Sorry...."

He rubbed his face with his free hand.

"Don't worry, I'll figure out a way to make you pay for it. There's caller ID on your cell for a reason. Look into it."

He hadn't called his grandmother since his return. Hell, he hadn't called to tell her he was leaving. That was unusual, since he was pretty good at letting her know where he was and what he was doing at any given time. Partly because she had a habit of coming down on him like a ton of bricks if he didn't.

Mostly because she deserved the consideration.

"How are you?"

He realized he didn't even know what time it was. He glanced at the clock on the bedside table. Just after four p.m.

"Elbow deep in cookie dough," she said.

He squinted.

"Christmas eve is tomorrow?"

Oh, hell....

The mere mention was enough to make him sick to his stomach. He wondered if it was possible to bow out of the festivities.

The idea was so sudden, it surprised him.

Never, ever, had he looked to get out of anything connected to Gram. It was just the nature of things.

"Jason and Jordan are flying in tomorrow morning. You'll be here, right?"

The vodka was beginning to dull his senses even further. "Yeah, sure, I'll be there."

Silence.

"Are you all right?" she asked quietly.

Now there was a question.

Was he all right?

"Yeah. I'm fine. I've just had a long day, that's all." Liar. "You need me to bring anything tomorrow?"

There was another heartbeat of silence that told him his grandmother knew he was lying, but was considering whether or not to call him on it.

"Just yourself."

"Okay. See you tomorrow then."

"Good."

He slowly disconnected and then sat for long minutes staring at his bedroom, noticing how foreign everything looked. He might as well have disconnected himself. Not by means of the telephone, but from everything familiar. He was accustomed to this sensation after coming home from long deployments. But this was different somehow. It went much deeper. Because this time, he wasn't looking for enemies around every corner. He was looking for Max…

16

FA-LA-LA-LA-LA-LA...fuck, fuck, fuck....

Max tried to conceal her personal twist on the song lyrics as her mom and aunt sang the true ones. She'd never much been one for holidays. Only now did that strike her as odd. Why didn't she like holidays? She supposed it wasn't so much that she didn't like them. Rather, it was because she failed to see the value in a single day when you should be living that way every day.

Of course, now she was giving serious consideration to hating them...

"Awww," her mom said, probably having unpacked yet another ornament with a sentimental story attached.

Max refrained from a physical eye roll, but allowed herself a mental one.

"Do you remember this, Maxi?"

She stepped up next to where Max hung the lights

on the artificial silver tree they'd had for years. Expecting to see her two-year-old handprint forever preserved in clay or something equally schmaltzy, she was unprepared for the photo Cindy held out.

She slowly reached out and took it, staring down at a picture of her and Jackson when they were fifteen? Sixteen? It was taken during winter and they both sat on hay bales, him wearing a Santa cap very similar to the one he'd had on at The Barracks, while her mother had stuck an antler headband on top of her head. They were both holding up peace signs...

She remembered that day so clearly she could nearly smell the straw.

She'd gone over to the Savage farm with her mom to deliver fruitcake to Jackson's grandmother, an annual tradition they had with several neighbors. She'd just stepped outside to look for Jackson...and gotten smacked on the side of the head with a snowball. Since she'd always given as good as she got, they'd indulged in an hour-long fight that finally found them in the barn together, right back at the spot where they first met....

Max sighed.

She recalled she had a snowball all ready in her hands and he'd grabbed her from behind, lifting her off the ground. She'd managed to struggle around and stuff the snow down the front of his flannel shirt. He'd pulled her so closely to him, she'd felt every inch of him...including his hard erection.

For a heart-pounding moment, she'd thought he'd kiss her. She'd prayed he would....

Then her mother had come outside with her camera and they'd jumped away from each other as if caught being very naughty.

Neither of them had breathed a word about the incident, or countless others just like it. And in many ways, Max had found it very easy to convince herself she'd imagined them. That her fantasies about Jackson wanting her were nothing but silly daydreams.

It would be so much easier if she held that same power now. But the past few days with Jackson had been so perfectly real....

She blinked back a sudden rush of tears.

She didn't know when her mother had placed the shot into a wreath frame to be hung on the tree, but she couldn't recall seeing it before.

She thrust it back at her. "I don't remember," she said.

The last thing she wanted was a replay of that morning. She'd soaked the shoulder of her mother's sweater for a good half hour before finally getting a hold of herself.

To her credit, Cindy hadn't pressed for the reason behind the waterworks. Likely, she'd thought it something connected to the job she'd been on. That was fine with Max. The more space she was allowed, the better.

"Of course, you remember," her mother said now about the ornament. "It was the day of that godawful snowstorm. It took us an hour to plow our way out of the driveway just so we could get up the road."

Now *that* she could honestly say she didn't remember. Likely because there were many times they'd done the same.

Her aunt sighed from behind them. "Cindy, remember when we all plotted to get Maxi and Jackson together?"

She nearly choked on her own spit, caught haplessly between grief and shock. "What? You guys did no such thing."

Her mother smiled. "Oh, yes, we did."

The living room of the old farmhouse was filled with boxes of holiday stuff. The aroma of cinnamon and pine from a wreath, and the soft sound of carols playing on the old radio in the corner added an otherworldly feel to the day.

Her aunt looked up from where she plucked garland and stockings from a box. "But, of course, no good matchmaking scheme would be worth a damn if we told the couple in question about it."

Max was having a hard time following the conversation. She knew her mom and aunt were telling the truth; while the two were known to exaggerate, they never outright lied.

"When?" she asked. "When did you guys do that?"

Her mom opened a box of huge, bright red bulbs. "Just before you two numbskulls signed up for the Corps."

Max blinked at her, then lifted a brow. "Numbskulls?"

"Yeah. Both of you were dumb as doorknobs then. Not a lick of sense between you."

Her aunt stepped up between them, reaching over Max's shoulder to adjust the lights she hung. "Never mind her. She never could tell a story to save her life...."

"Me? You always want to jump straight to the punchline."

"You're talking about a joke, sweetie."

"Same difference." Her mother looked back at her. "What I mean is that neither one of you had a brain in your head when it came to the other. There Jackson went skipping off to the Marines because his big brother did, and there you went, following right along after him. Just like you always did."

Max tried to wrap her head around what her mother was saying. "I didn't sign up because of Jax."

They both stared at her.

Is that what they truly thought? That she'd become a Marine because of some sort of unrequited love for a guy who never even looked at her that way? "I didn't. I signed up because of Grandpa."

"Uh-huh," her mother said in that way that always grated against her nerves.

"People don't become Marines because of some-one else," Max said flatly. "A Marine is born a Marine...."

"Anyway, that's neither here nor there," her aunt said, quickly, always the peacemaker. "What we're talking about is that time we set you both to work up at the General Store together."

Max squinted at her. "You did not."

Her aunt smiled. "Did so."

She half expected her mother to stick her tongue out at her.

"You certainly don't think it was a coincidence that Jackson was hired the day after you were, do you?" her aunt asked.

Max thought back to the time. It had been a few months before graduation and both of them had been looking for extra cash. She was glad when a Help Wanted sign was posted at the General Store. She'd gone in to inquire and had instantly gotten a cash-ier's position.

Then Jackson had walked through the door the following day, apparently hired on as a stock han-dler, and her heart had twirled in her chest. Oh, she saw him at school all the time, and at various school and community related events, but outside brief snatches of time like the day of the snowball fight, they hadn't spoken much. But at the General Store...

She caught herself smiling in bittersweet remembrance.

Sometimes he'd bring her a muffin from a batch his grandmother had made. Sometimes she'd give him half her sandwich at lunch and the two of them would sit on the back loading dock, feet hanging over the side, talking about everything and nothing, sometimes leaning into each other and smiling...

She glanced to find her mother and aunt sharing a secret smile that wasn't so secret.

This time she didn't try to hide her eye roll.

"You two are pathetic," she said. "You both should look into having the rose-tint permanently removed from your corneas. Really, it's quite sickening."

Her mother sighed. "Yes, well, that attempt didn't work out as planned, did it? You never even went to the prom."

Max winced. Like she needed the reminder of that old bit of scar tissue on top of what she felt now.

"That's because he asked Jennifer Wills," she whispered.

Her aunt made a growling sound. "I swear, Cindy, you're as dense as a cow patty sometimes."

"What?"

Max finished putting up the lights and dropped her arms to her sides. "I'm getting more coffee. Either of you want any?"

She walked away without waiting for an answer.

"Why would you want coffee when there's perfectly good eggnog in the fridge?" her aunt asked.

Max entered the kitchen and closed the swinging door. She leaned against the counter and rubbed her closed eyelids, thankful for the brief moment of silence.

Her head ached and her heart felt as if it might explode. She hadn't been able to eat more than a few tasteless bites or drink more than a few sips of anything since her return. A voice told her she should try, it would help her feel better. But the thought was enough to make her feel sick to her stomach.

This was so incredibly stupid.

Stupid or not, she found she was crying…again.

Of course, it didn't help that she was rooming with two of the biggest romantics in human history. No matter what happened, what they went through, what ugliness her aunt and mother encountered, their staunch belief in love was…

Nauseating.

How in the hell was she going to survive the next two days closed up in the house with them during the holidays?

How in the hell was she going to survive living with herself?

She stared outside at the cloudy day, one of what she knew would be an endless winter stream of them. She hated this time of year. Short days, little sunshine. She should go somewhere warm.

She watched fat snowflakes swirl in the frigid breeze and her breath caught, another memory coming to her.

She'd been four, maybe five. Her father had left her and her mother blessedly alone for a few days, disappearing as he had a habit of doing every now and again. Her mother had always been happier during those times. Baking and playing games with her.

On this particular winter day, she had been standing at the window of their dingy little one-bedroom house on the outskirts of town and Max had joined her, trying to loop her arms around her hips. Her mother had caught her wrists and held them there.

"Look, Maxi, faeries have come down to visit you. If you close your eyes and wish for something really, really hard, they'll make sure it comes true."

Now, so many years later, she found herself closing her eyes and making a wish she didn't even dare acknowledge to herself.

She felt a moment of sheer longing, then opened her eyes to find nothing had changed. She was still standing in the kitchen of her aunt's farmhouse. She still hurt. And the two women in the other room still were laughing.

Stupid. When had any of her mother's wishes ever come true?

She grabbed her coat off the mudroom hook and her mother's car keys and left the house, the only destination in mind being anywhere far away from there....

17

JACKSON WOKE FEELING as if his head was an orange and someone was squeezing it for juice. He could have told them not to bother, there was none to be had.

He sat upright, blinking hard, something stuck to his cheek. He reached up and peeled a piece of paper from his skin then looked at the kitchen table in front of him. It was littered with items from the project he'd been consumed with since yesterday. The sheet he'd been sleeping on was a list of deceased team members he'd procured from Pegasus, along with their contact numbers, family names and insurance forms the next of kin would need to fill out to claim death benefits.

He ran his hands over his face then pushed from the table, nearly stumbling over where Cleo was curled sleeping against his foot.

He grumbled an apology and stepped over her,

going to the bathroom where he splashed water over his face. For long moments he stood staring at his reflection in the mirror. He looked like holy hell. Worse than that, even. He hadn't shaved in days and looked like he'd been on a ten-day bender. He opened the medicine cabinet and took out his razor and shaving cream, then reached over to switch on the shower.

Ten minutes later, he felt and looked somewhat more human.

Whatever that meant...

Was that someone knocking?

Rubbing the towel against his neck, he peered around the open doorway. Who in the hell would be looking for him now?

He tucked the towel around his hips as he headed for the door, then stood staring at the one person he'd last expected to see, but most wanted to...

Max.

MAXINE BLINKED ONCE, then twice, her mouth instantly flooding at the sight of Jackson standing before her in nothing but a fluffy white towel.

She swallowed hard.

"Hi," she said, feeling ridiculously shy.

Shy? She wasn't shy. And the two of them had done things that would make the gods blush.

So why was she shy now?

"Hey," he said.

He looked around her, as if expecting someone else to be with her.

"Come in."

"Thanks."

After leaving her aunt's house, with no destination in mind other than to drive as far away as fast as possible, she was surprised to find herself ultimately parked in the lot of The Barracks. All things considered, she supposed she should've expected it. Jackson had been on her mind so heavily it was probably natural she would unconsciously seek him out, look for answers to questions that haunted her like the winter wind blowing behind her back.

He closed the door behind her and she realized she was standing in nearly the same spot she had been the first night he'd taken her up there. The night he'd reached to take her coat...and had stripped her of much, much more. And given her more than she would have ever dared dream.

This time, she shrugged out of her coat on her own volition rather than pretending it protected her from anything.

She caught her gaze plastered to his hard abs and swallowed hard again, her fingertips itching to reach out and touch him. He stood so close, the soap from his shower filled her nose. Yet he remained so far away, the frigid cold outside had nothing on him.

Jackson Savage had always been hotly attractive. Her mother had liked to say he was like a blazing fire to the chilled female masses. They would always be drawn to his heat. She'd seen that firsthand, beginning with the dating candidates that lined up, giving him a neverending selection of companions.

And now she felt as if she'd gotten so close to the fire, she'd been burned.

"I'm, uh, just going to go get dressed," he said.

Max didn't realize her gaze had dropped lower, taking in what was hidden beneath the towel, until he spoke.

She blinked up at him. "Oh. Yeah."

Though he said he was leaving, he still stood in front of her.

Was that need she saw in his eyes? Or was it her own need reflected in the blue depths.

"I'll be right back."

She nodded. "I heard you the first time."

He offered a shadow of a smile and then he finally turned.

She made no secret of watching him go because there was no reason to. Not only because no one was looking, but because it was obvious how she felt about him. It was useless to hide it now.

The question was, what did she do with it?

"You can make some coffee if you want. There are grounds in the fridge, filters above the sink."

It took her a moment to register the words coming from the bedroom.

"Sure."

She went into the kitchen and readied a pot to brew, then turned toward the dining room. The black cat she'd seen earlier was in the middle of the table, giving herself a tongue bath. She spared Max a long, questioning gaze, then dismissed her and returned to her previously scheduled activity.

Max mentally shook her head. She'd had pets growing up, but they'd been relegated to outdoors. Seeing one sitting in the middle of the kitchen table took some getting used to.

In an effort to do that, she moved closer and reached out to scratch—it was Cleo, right?—Cleo behind the ears. The cat purred so loudly she smiled.

Then her gaze caught on a bit of familiar letterhead. As she scratched the cat, she leaned closer to read it. Pegasus.

Jackson couldn't possibly still be working for them? Not after all they'd been through? Not after telling her he wouldn't be returning.

The cat forgotten, Max sifted through the papers, trying to make sense of them. Cleo jumped down from the table and sprawled out across her feet, her meow capturing Max's attention.

Max looked over her shoulder to find Jackson standing barefoot, wearing jeans and buttoning a denim shirt, his hair still damp.

"What's this?" she asked.

He moved to stand next to her. Again his scent nearly overwhelmed her.

"A project I'm working on."

"Project?"

He started gathering the documents together but said nothing.

"You're not still working for them?"

"What?" He paused. "No. No, I'm not."

She crossed her arms over her chest. "I don't understand, then."

"I'm contacting the family members of our fallen teammates," he said so quietly she nearly didn't hear him.

A heartbeat of silence passed. Then another.

Wow.

"I stopped by Pegasus on a hunch yesterday and was proven right. They hadn't contacted next of kin yet and had no plans to do so until after the holidays."

"What?" Max's voice was a whisper.

He stacked the papers neatly and then moved them out of the way. "Yeah."

They both stood for long moment, neither of them saying anything.

Max couldn't fathom anyone not telling her mother and aunt that she had died during combat as soon as the news was available. What were they thinking? She'd like to believe their motives were well-meaning, that they didn't want to cast a dark cloud over the holidays, but she suspected their motivation was much more selfish.

She was having a hard time wrapping her mind around the information. She dropped into the nearest chair and sat staring at the papers. The past two days she had been so wrapped up in herself, her own selfish emotions, she hadn't even thought about taking up what Jackson was doing.

"Would you like a cup of coffee?" he asked.

"What?" She hadn't realized he'd moved until she saw him taking cups out of the cupboard. "Oh. Yes, please."

"Still cream, no sugar?"

"Um, yeah."

She brought the pile of documents closer, staring at a list of names she'd committed to memory. "Have you spoken to anyone yet?"

He placed a cup at her elbow then took the seat across from her. "No." He took a long sip of his coffee. "I wanted to make sure everything was in order first. I want to be able to tell them what insurance would be covering and to what degree, as well as how long the process would take."

"Everything Pegasus should be doing."

He ran his hand through his hair. "Yeah. Essentially." He drew in a deep breath and let it out. "What I'm trying to figure out is whether I should do it today, or I don't know…"

Whereas Pegasus's motives where in question, Jackson's heart was in the exact right place. Of course, it always had been.

"Just after Christmas is soon enough."

His eyes lifted to meet hers. In them she saw deep gratitude, along with relief mixed with grief. "Yeah."

"I talked to Taylor this morning. She goes home from the hospital today."

He nodded, but she wondered if he heard her. Still, she was sure he was aware of their fallen member's recovery.

She put the papers back down. "Would you like some help?"

Again, he didn't appear to hear her.

"You know, notifying the families? If we split it up, we can be doubly effective. And everyone will know as soon as possible."

He sat back. "Yeah, I'd like that. Thanks."

"Sure."

Silence fell between them.

"Max, about what happened—"

"Jackson, I was hoping you might be able to answer—"

They spoke at the same time and then laughed awkwardly, avoiding each other's gaze.

"You first," he said.

She shook her head. "You know how I feel about that 'ladies first' crap."

"It has nothing to do with you being a lady."

She stared at him.

"Okay, maybe just a little." His smile was a bit warmer. "But it's mostly because I'm a coward."

"Coward? That's one word I'd never use to describe you."

"Maybe it should be the first."

She squinted at him, more than a little concerned. "I'm not sure I'm following you."

He shifted uncomfortably, then pushed from his chair altogether. "More coffee?"

"I have yet to take a drink from this one."

He moved to the kitchen. She pinpointed the avoidance technique for what it was. But she wasn't about to let the subject drop.

He came back to the table but didn't sit down.

"Explain, please," she said.

He slowly unbuttoned his left cuff and began rolling the sleeve up his corded forearm. "Isn't there a question you wanted to ask me?"

"It can wait."

He seemed overly concerned with rolling up his other sleeve.

"Jax?"

He began to turn from her and she got to her feet, stepping into his path.

"Uh-huh. I need for you to answer the question."

His gaze was hard and she nearly flinched from the change. She forced herself to hold her ground. "Leave it, Max," he said.

She shook her head. "No."

They stood like that for long moments, the sound of the cat lapping water out of a nearby bowl and the refrigerator humming the only things breaking the silence.

She wasn't going to leave it. It was out of the question.

"Then leave me..."

18

JACKSON REGRETTED THE WORDS the moment they were out. But once they were, he couldn't bring himself to retract them.

Max looked like someone had just pulled a weapon on her. And he supposed he had, in a manner of speaking.

He wanted, no, he *needed* her to take a step back. Leave him be. Let him figure out what in the hell was going on inside his head and then map a way out.

"No," she said, point blank.

He squinted at her.

"I'm not going to leave. I've—" She gestured with her hands, as if trying to find the words to best express her thoughts. "These past two days I've done this your way. I've allowed you to take the lead, set the pace, decide what was or wasn't said." She shook her head. "No more."

"Max…"

"No. You've said quite enough already, thank you." She resembled a lit match, her red hair seeming even brighter as sparks ignited her green eyes. "What you don't understand is that you've said plenty by saying nothing at all. But I know you, Jackson Savage. Probably better than anyone else in the world…"

He'd give her that.

He crossed his arms, finding his mood lightening as he watched her give herself over to a good fit.

"You say you're a coward. I say you're one of the bravest men I've ever met. It's because of you that all of your team members made it out. It's because of you that any of us did."

He grimaced and looked away. She knew he was thinking about those who didn't.

"Oh, no, you don't, buster. Don't you dare tune out on me again. I won't have it."

They both glanced at where her hand rested against his arm in order to redirect and maintain his attention.

And boy did she ever have it.

He glanced up into her eyes to find the emotion in them had shifted…but not lessened.

Damn, but she was beautiful. Everything about her was so alive, so intriguing, so very, very sexy…

Jackson's gaze slid from her eyes to her mouth,

then down to where her breasts heaved under her clingy cotton top.

"I'm up here, Savage," she said.

If there was a slight wispiness to her voice, her steely expression didn't show it. But he could tell she wasn't angry at him; she felt their chemistry as intensely as he did.

And boy did he ever feel it. Merely being this close to her made him want to kiss her senseless, slide his hand up her top and down her pants, stroke her until she gasped in pure bliss....

He swallowed hard.

Whatever Max felt, she'd always felt to the max. Maximum Maxine is what the guys had called her. And they were right. You didn't mess with Max unless you expected to get beaten, or to fight to the death....

The stupid, off-the-cuff thought shifted his thoughts back to Africa.

And brought him right back to where this all started....

He leveled a loaded gaze at her. "Forget it, Mc-Guire. It's not going to work."

"Work? What are you talking about? What, is this some sort of game? Is that what you think?" She squinted at him. "Oh, wait. Is that what it was? You. Me. Us. A game?"

Jackson set his jaw. "Back off, Max."

"Or else what? What can you possibly do to me

that you haven't already done?" He blinked at the catch in her voice. "Tell me, because I can't possibly imagine anything hurting as much as this."

Jackson felt as if she'd reached her hand directly inside his chest and tore his heart out.

"What? Surely you know your silence has been killing me? That the instant you turned away from me in Africa, it was like you had stuck your serated knife into my chest and twisted?"

He raised his hand. "Max, please…."

"No, Jackson. Answer me."

What could he possibly say? That he'd been so wrapped up in his own emotions he hadn't taken hers into consideration? Besides, what did his knowing now change except to make him feel worse than he already did? Didn't it just reinforce the decision he'd already made?

Her expression switched from anger to…was that shock?

"Oh my God. You didn't know, did you? You had no clue that I loved you," she whispered.

He glanced away.

She shifted slightly. "Wow."

Silence filled the room as he guessed she digested the information.

"You really had no idea?"

Jackson grimaced and paced away then back again. "What difference does it make, Max? This, whatever's happening, happened, between us, it can't go anywhere."

She raised her hand to stop him. "Happening. Not happened. And it's been happening since the first day we met in your grandmother's dusty old barn."

He stared at her, immediately transported back to that day.

"You hated my guts."

She smiled almost sadly. "No, Jax. I loved you. And I love you still."

Was it possible for one man's heart to hold so much emotion? So much pain? So much confusion?

He wasn't sure. And wouldn't have been surprised if his had burst from what he was feeling now.

"Yeah, tell me about it," she said, sighing. "What, you think I like realizing that I've wasted so much time."

She moved away from him this time, standing with her back to him. His attention was riveted to her.

"I moved from relationship to relationship, guy to guy, never realizing I unconsciously measured them all against you," she said quietly. "Not until the last one."

She turned toward him.

"That's what I'm doing here, Jackson, the reason I came back to Colorado. I had to see if what Matt said was true."

The sound of another man's name on her lips twisted his gut. "Who in the hell is Matt?"

She gestured restlessly. "Matt, James, Bob, what does it matter? They're all the same guy. They're all not you."

He tried but failed to follow her bullet train of thought. What was she saying? Was she trying to tell him she'd been with a lot of guys? He rubbed the back of his neck.

"Anyway, about Matt. He was a nice guy. They all were. He loved me. But when I couldn't tell him I felt the same, you know what he said?"

He wasn't sure if her question was rhetorical so he remained silent, trying to oust the image of her lying in bed with another man from his head.

"He told me he couldn't think of anything he'd like more than to be with me. Only I wasn't with him. Not truly."

Jackson scratched the back of his head in irritation, then stared at her. The expression on her face was captivating; her pupils were large, her lips were slightly parted, and her breathing seemed shallow.

"He said I needed to think twice about getting involved with anyone, because obviously, I was still in love with someone else. Someone I had never gotten over. And until I did, well, it was unfair of me to lead on some other poor sucker who'd never stand a chance."

"He was good with words, your guy Mark."

"Matt."

"Whatever."

She smiled slightly, which only served to annoy him further.

"So who's this guy you never got over then? No, wait, don't tell me. Joe."

"Who?"

He shook his head, his attempt at humor failing even to amuse him.

"Seriously?" she whispered.

He watched her step closer to him, completely mesmerized. What was this woman doing to him? And why was he incapable of stopping her?

"You really want to know?" she asked, standing so close to him now that when she inhaled, the tips of her breasts brushed his chest.

He tried to steel himself against her, but failed.

"No answer?"

She leaned forward, her breath mingling with his, her scent filling his nose, her mouth so damn tempting he ached with the need to kiss her....

"That man is you, Jackson Savage. The one I'm in love with? The one I never got over? The one I can't move on from? You, you and...you."

Her voice grew progressively softer so the last word was little more than a hush of air.

As if of their own volition, his fingers curved around her slender neck, the heel of his hand against her jaw, the pad of his thumb rubbing against her full bottom lip.

Then he kissed her.

Sweet heaven.

Torturous hell.

Her lips were like wine soaked plums, both in texture and potency. He appeared to have caught her off guard and she stood, transfixed as he pressed his lips against hers once, then again, tasting her with his tongue before claiming them more fully, begging for permission to enter the intoxicating depths of her mouth.

She made a sound somewhere between a sigh and a moan and leaned into him, her eyelids drifting closed, her hands resting against his hips as if she needed the leverage.

It was impossible to believe this was the same warrior he'd served with on the front lines. The same girl he'd grown up with.

He knew her better than anyone else in the world.

Yet he knew her not at all.

She shifted against him, rubbing against his rock hard erection and sending his blood rushing to his groin.

Just like that, the world disappeared and all that existed was her, this kiss, her body. Her love.

He closed his eyes tightly and pressed his nose against hers.

"I can't do this," he said.

He ordered himself to release her, to let go, but everything refused to obey.

"I don't want this," he continued.

She began to pull away, but he refused to let her go.

"But, damn it, I need it…"

_19_

MAX WAS HOPELESSLY caught somewhere between bliss and grief. She felt raw, exposed and so very vulnerable. The last of her defenses were down and she had no clue how to put them back up against this one man who threatened to destroy her entirely.

He wanted this.

Sex? Was he talking strictly sex?

He'd remained so impassively silent during her explanation, she didn't know what to think.

And right this minute, given the way he was kissing her, his hands roaming over her body, she was finding it impossible to think of anything else at all.

His mouth demanded compliance and she gave it.

His hands caressed her breasts and she shivered.

His eyes looked into hers and her lungs refused air. Her heart threatened to break clean in two.

Somewhere she drew the strength to push him away. "Please, don't."

His expression was dark as she wiped her damp lips with the back of her hand.

"What's the matter, Max? Isn't this what you wanted?"

He took her hand and pressed it against his hard erection.

She left it there for a long moment, imagining she could feel his pulse in the long, solid length of him.

Finally, she jerked back.

"No. That's not what I wanted, Jackson."

"Then what *do* you want? Because right now I'm having a hell of a time figuring it out."

"Honesty," she whispered. "I want honesty."

She wanted her best friend back.

"Well, baby, this is as honest as it gets with me."

He drew her to him and kissed her hard.

Need and fear twisted and turned within her. Not fear of him, but fear of herself. She wanted, needed, him in a way she'd never needed another. But he'd just told her he didn't want anything beyond this, this moment. The passion.

While she wanted the whole nine yards.

She tried to pull away, or thought she did.... Instead, she discovered she was hungrily returning his attentions, er mouth wildly kissing his, her hands boldly grasping and clutching....

Pure physical need saturated her every cell.

Jackson shoved his hand up her shirt, cupping her

breast through her bra, fastening his mouth to her nipple through the fabric before sliding his thumb under the bottom and lifting until his tongue met with the ultra sensitive bit.

Max reached for his jeans, unable to unfasten them quick enough as he did the same with hers. Then he was lifting her to the table. She began to wrap her legs around him but instead he laid her back. She moved to object…until she felt his tongue on her inner thigh.

The air rushed from her lungs.

Oh…

The word wound around her mind in one long, unbroken strand as fire licked along her skin along with flicks of his tongue. His fingers lightly probed her then opened her damp flesh to the cool air, causing delicious shivers to trickle over her body. But they were nothing compared to the tidal wave of sensation she experienced when he ran his tongue again her clit.

She gasped, her back arching off the table.

Jackson splayed his hand against her trembling stomach, holding her still as he fastened his lips around her and suckled.

She came instantly in a series of intense, womb wracking shudders he drew out by continuing his attentions.

Then before the last one subsided, he was sheathed and sliding into her.

Yes.…

JACKSON'S DESIRE TO please Max knew no bounds. Even in his heightened sense of awareness—not only of her sexually, but of his own need to keep himself emotionally distant—he wanted to bring her a pleasure she hadn't known before. Wanted to watch her mouth bow open, her eyes go dark. He wanted to listen to her moan low in the back of her throat as if trying to contain it but failing.

But when it came to emotional distance, all bets were off the instant he dipped into her hot heat. Sex and emotion seemed to fuse with each other until he swore his heart was about to burst with...

Love?

Without a familiar compass to help guide him, he had no idea he was so close to coming. All he could do was grasp her hips and slide into her again, giving himself over to the incredible sensation that joined him with her.

What seemed like long minutes later, he cracked open his eyes to see her waching him.

Dear Lord, what had he gotten himself into...?

HOURS LATER, MAX LAY on her side in Jackson's bed, his hot body curved against hers. She'd drifted off for a few minutes and suspected he was fully asleep now if his deep, even breathing was any indication. She really needed to get home, but she couldn't bring herself to move. Not because she was content, but because she was afraid if she left the bed, she might find her way back to it.

There were moments over the past couple of hours when she swore Jackson had opened up to her, when she'd felt a connection to him unlike any before. Then he'd get that shuttered look again and her heart would break.

She had no idea what was going through his mind. She couldn't draw a bead on him, no matter how hard she tried.

And now she was strangely physically sated, not to mention mentally exhausted, from the efforts.

As well as an emotional mess.

How could he speak so eloquently to her with his body, his touch? Yet keep her blocked from the rest?

Movement.

Her heart skipped a beat as his hand budged on her hip. Despite the cold temperature outside, inside it was warm, so all they'd needed was a top sheet, and even that was bunched around their waists. She caught her breath as he moved his hand from the sheet to slide under it, dipping over her hip and not coming to a stop until it rested between her thighs. Against her better judgment, she opened to him.

Judgment? Hadn't she proven she had none when it came to Jackson Savage?

She closed her eyes and drew in a slow breath through her mouth. Was he still sleeping, his movement something automatic? He stroked her, sending sensation swirling. Um, no. He was definitely awake.

Max spread her thighs farther, allowing him freer

access even as she arched toward him. She shivered at the feel of his erection pressing against her.

When they'd made love before (and she was certain they had made love), she had let herself go, given herself over to the sweet bliss of their connection.

With her back to him, she decided she'd do that again now, just allow herself to feel her own emotions, forget his, forget this would be their last time together....

That mere thought wound the ball of sadness tighter in her chest. She swallowed the tears and took a deep breath, reaching between her own thighs to touch his hand where he stroked her, then beyond, wrapping her fingers around his hard length.

His breath hissed into her ear, feeding her boldness. She guided him to rest between her damp folds, shivering in anticipation as she held him there, stroking him even as she rocked her hips, covering him with her need.

Jackson moved, reached behind him to grab a condom, moving back just enough to put it on as she better positioned herself. A moment later, the tip rested against her slick entrance and paused there. She held her breath in anticipation before forcing admission, sliding back until he was in to the hilt.

She sighed in sweet surrender, shimmering light filling her to overflowing.

Yes...

Jackson withdrew then sank in again, heightening her need. She reached back, grasping his bottom even as she tilted her hips to take him deeper still.

Every part of him surrounded her, saturated her until she no longer recognized herself as an individual but as a hungry entity only he could feed.

He nuzzled her shoulder, then her neck, causing ribbons of sensation to unfurl down her body, teasing her nipples, tickling her stomach. She arched back, seeking his lips, finding them, kissing him deeply, welcoming his tongue in her mouth.

Oh, how very much she loved him.

He cupped her face so very gently, his strokes matching those of his fingers as they moved down to her breasts, rolling her aching nipples between his fingers before continuing down her trembling belly, claiming her from the front as well as from behind.

Max moaned into his mouth, unsure if she could possibly withstand the pleasure possessing every part of her. She was sure she would combust at any moment, fearing it while at the same time welcoming it.

Though they had known each other for years, it seemed everything was fresh, new. And she so yearned to explore everything about him, them, together.

He slid his hands to grasp her hips, halting her restless grinding as he thrust deeply inside her.

Max broke their kiss and moaned.

She slid her hand between her legs to where they were joined, stroking his dripping hardness as he drove into her again.

Yes.

She entwined her hands in the sheets, holding on, trying to stay grounded even as she catapulted to a place somewhere high above them, floating, flying.

"I love you," she said, somewhere between a whisper and a moan, knowing as she did so, truer words had never been uttered.

But at the same time understanding she would never say them to him again.

Darkness mingled with light as his thrusts became harder, faster. It was as if he, too, shared that same understanding, trying to punish her for giving him something he was incapable of returning.

20

Christmas Eve

THE SETTING WAS RIGHT: fat, fluffy snowflakes floated on the cold air, carols played on the stereo; the scent of ginger from earlier baking and of a ham now roasting teased the senses, presents were under the tree beckoning to be unwrapped.

Yet, somehow, Max was unable to summon up the spirit needed to enjoy any of it, including her French vanilla roast coffee.

It was nine p.m. and she stood in front of the living room window staring outside in the direction of the Savage farm, her mind far away from what was happening in the room behind her. She kept replaying what had happened earlier after she had uttered those three words...

The joy, the sorrow, the chaos....

Sweaty and sated, she had curved against Jackson, feeling his physical nearness, mourning his emotional distance....

Then he'd rolled away from her abruptly. "I've got to go."

"Jax..." She had lifted to a sitting position, self-conscious despite the intimacy they'd shared as she gathered the sheet around her. "I..."

She what?

He'd barely spared her a glance as he pulled on his jeans.

"Look at me. Please."

He appeared prepared to ignore her request.

And she almost wished he would have when she received his stony gaze.

It was all too easy to believe, in that one moment, that he had never felt anything for her ever.

That they had never been friends.

She'd bitten her bottom lip, feeling more vulnerable than a single leaf clinging to a tree branch: one stiff wind and she'd be lost forever.

"I just wanted to say you're not alone. Whatever you're going through?" she'd said softly. "I'm here. For an ear. Advice. Or just quiet companionship."

He pulled on socks, a T-shirt and his flannel shirt.

"You're not responsible for Africa," she'd whispered.

He hadn't said anything for a long moment, then he repeated, "I've got to go."

And she'd let him.

She stayed put few minutes longer, listening as the apartment door closed behind him. Then heartache had pushed her from his bed, propelling her home where she'd stood under the shower spray until the water grew cold, feeling numb to the core long before it had.

She knew he loved her. She could feel it.

Why, then, was he denying it?

"Maxi?" her mother said behind her.

She swallowed hard and turned to face Cindy, smiling.

"You okay?"

She nodded, incapable of words just then.

She was not going to cry on her mom's shoulder. Not again.

"The ham's just about done. You hungry?"

She shook her head.

Cindy considered her for a long moment. "Okay. Maybe just a cookie for now? Come on. Come sit with me next to the fire."

She hesitated.

"Don't worry, I'm not going to ask any question you're not ready to answer. I just want to share a story with you."

A story.

She looked around. "Where's Aunt Theresa?"

"In the kitchen. Come on."

Cindy led the way toward the two comfortable wing chairs in front of the fireplace. Max reluctantly followed and sat opposite her mother, her gaze seeking out and getting lost in the lick of the flames around the logs. She was aware of Cindy putting a plate of cookies on the table between them, but she didn't acknowledge them.

At least, until her mom put a gingerbread man in her right hand.

"I remember these were always your favorite. Ever since you were little and got into a plate of them when I wasn't looking." She smiled sweetly. "You ate the whole dozen. I was afraid you were going to burst." A quiet laugh. "Of course, you probably had more on you than in you, but still...."

Max had heard the story before. Every Christmas, in fact. But somehow she never tired of it. It was a tradition of sorts, sharing these memories.

Of course, it wasn't usually this quiet on Christmas Eve. Traditionally, Theresa's family stayed the night and the house was filled with the creak of someone on the stairs, water running, laughter and glasses and silverware clinking.

Not this year, though. This year it was just the three of them.

And Max was grateful for it, even if a part of her was a little sad that things were changing, and not always for the better.

"I wanted to talk to you about your dad...."

Without realizing it, Max had taken a bite of her

cookie. It instantly turned to the texture of sawdust in her mouth.

She put the remainder down and coughed, using her coffee to wash down the mouthful.

"Yes, I know," her mother said. "It's not normally a topic open for discussion, is it?"

Discussion? Her father was rarely brought up. Understandably so.

Which made her doubly curious why Cindy wanted to talk about him now.

"You don't have to say anything," her mom said. "It's just that…" She stared into the fire, her eyes taking on a faraway look. "I'm watching you struggle… No, I've watched you struggle for so many years now. But more so recently, I think, right?"

Cindy searched her face with a smile.

Max stared into the depths of her coffee cup.

"I first met Claude at a harvest dance when I was fifteen."

Max raised her brows. The only time she had ever heard her father mentioned was in negative terms. To listen to her mom speak of him now, and in such a fond tone of voice, inspired mixed feelings. She wanted to encourage her to say more, and yet hold up her hand to stop her.

Instead, she remained silent.

"He was three years older than me and my friends. It means nothing now, but back then…" She sighed. "He seemed so…worldly."

Her father? Worldly?

"And handsome?" She made a humming sound that surprised her. "I thought my heart was going to burn a hole through the soles of my feet every time he looked at me."

Max's stomach felt lined with lead. All she could remember is watching her father raise his fist to her mother. Often.

She winced at the memory.

"You're thinking about the bad times, aren't you?" Cindy asked. She glanced down into her mug of eggnog. "I'm so sorry about that, Maxi. Sorry you ever had to see the bad."

"I'm sorry you had to live it."

Their gazes met. Max realized neither of them had said words similar to those in all these years.

"I don't want you to ever blame yourself," Cindy said.

"But if it wasn't for me, you would never have stayed."

"Is that what you think?"

She nodded.

"Honey, if it weren't for you, I would have missed out on the greatest love of my life."

Tears poked her eyes.

"What I'm trying to say here is, things weren't always bad between your dad and I. Things were actually quite beautiful in the beginning."

"I'm not sure I want to hear this."

"I'm sure you need to."

"Please, Mom...."

Silence fell between them.

Somewhere in the kitchen a pot banged. Her aunt was probably setting the kitchen table for midnight dinner, a longtime tradition Theresa insisted on even though there were only three of them this year, compared to the houseful they usually had. Although judging by the amount of food the two women had cooked, all of Colorado Springs could have been coming for dinner. The only concession to the smaller gathering was the setting of the kitchen table instead of the large dining room one, where absences would be too obvious.

"I'm so very sorry," her mother said.

"Mom."

"No, Maxi, please. I need to say this."

She bit her bottom lip to keep from objecting more.

"I've been watching you lately. Something's changed in you. Something that's allowed me to see you in a new light, perhaps help put things into perspective...."

She tightened her hands around her cup, the contents of which had long grown cold.

"I know you don't view your aunt and me favorably. I know you think we're nothing but a couple of old fools."

"No, I..."

Her mother's raised brow stopped her from uttering an untruth.

"Okay." She softened her words with a small smile. "Maybe I do think your rose-tinted glasses are too thick, just a little."

Cindy laughed. "A little? You've compared them to aquarium glass in the past."

"Yeah, I have, haven't I?" She took a sip. "Sorry."

"No, you're not."

They shared a fond glance.

"And that's okay. That's you. It's what life—your life, my life—has made you."

Max narrowed her eyes.

"There's nothing wrong with that. However..."

Max waited.

"There's so very much more I'm afraid you're not seeing, that your experiences have prevented you from seeing...."

She grimaced. "What? Like love?"

Her mother smiled brightly, warmly. "Yes."

She put her cup down. "Sorry. Not interested."

She hated saying it so abruptly, her words like a slap that knocked the happiness out of her mother's face. But she had to.

Cindy grimaced. "You'll excuse me for saying you're dumb as a doorknob then?"

"No."

She shrugged. "Then don't. Because you are."

Max pulled her knees up to her chest and wrapped her arms around them.

"Baby, don't you see? That's what we're put on this earth to do. To love. Without it, well, nothing makes sense. And you deny all the beauty. It's almost like tramping on a flower instead of stopping to smell it."

"I never was a flower girl."

Her mother laughed. "No, you weren't, were you?"

Max smiled and rested her cheek against her legs, looking into the fire.

"And now those flowers are men."

She lifted her head again. "What?"

"You heard me. I'm afraid you're viewing men the same way you would flowers: as unnecessary. Worthless."

"No, I'm not…."

"May I finish?"

"Depends. Will it take long?"

Her mother's face fell.

She took a deep breath. "Sorry."

"What I'm trying to say, Maxi, is that the lessons your life, and my life, have taught you… It's not to distrust all men. It's to trust them until they give you reason not to."

Her ribs bit into her heart as she remembered Jackson's face earlier. He'd given her reason not to trust him. Oh, he hadn't raised a hand to her, as her father had to her mother. But he'd hit her with an emotional blow that left a mark just as lasting.

The kitchen door opened. "Girls? You planning on helping?"

Max and her mother sat like that for a few moments more. Then Cindy got up, rested her hand briefly on top of Max's head, smoothing her hair back. Max closed her eyes, absorbing the emotions stirred by the soothing gesture.

"Think about it, baby? Please? Love isn't something you fight against—it's something you surrender to. That's the one lesson your father never learned. I'd hate for you to inherit that legacy."

Max's heart nearly stopped at the comparison. It was a vivid one to be sure. And she knew she wasn't talking about her father's violent acts, but rather what may have been at the heart of them....

"There was one thing I learned from my experiences," her mother whispered, leaning closer to her ear. "It's not to shun love, but to look for it. You know why? Because my love for you proves there's a neverending supply so long as you know where to look." She smiled at her. "I pray that you find that."

21

JACKSON'S ONLY PLAN was to avoid everything and everyone for as long as he possibly could.

He shoveled the parking lot and the front of The Barracks for the third time that night, even though the falling snow covered the path as quickly as he uncovered it. He leaned on the shovel in front of the door, considering the fat snowflakes. The street was quiet, most everybody home for the night, where they should be.

Where he should be.

Gram had called no fewer than five times before he'd finally taken her call, telling her he had to work that night.

"Bullhockey. Your brother's here with his girl. We're waiting on you."

He'd told her he'd be there most likely in the morning.

The longer he put off seeing his brother, the better.

The more he pushed Max out of his mind, the better yet.

While his delaying his visit to the farm was effective with dealing with Jason, avoiding Max... Well, merely thinking her name made him wince, remembering her face when he'd climbed out of bed earlier and practically run away from her.

It had taken nearly every ounce of willpower he had to drag himself away from her. Had he not summoned it, he might very well still be lying in that bed with her.

He was surprised by his immediate arousal at the thought.

Damn it, why was this happening now? Why had Max come back and opened fire on his plans? Why had he given himself over to base physical needs when it came to his best friend?

He winced again, recognizing the harshness of his thoughts. But when bullets came to firing, that was the barrel through which they were shot, wasn't it? He blamed himself.

Hell, he wasn't sure of anything anymore. Except that everything he'd thought he'd wanted? Everything he'd been working toward? It had been completely obliterated.

The door opened. He stepped out of the way to allow an unfamiliar patron of the bar to walk outside, watching as the man hunkered down into his coat and headed for the parking lot.

"Merry Christmas," the stranger said.

Jackson returned the greeting, wondering what was so merry about it.

He tapped the shovel on the ground and went inside, tucking it out of the way before shrugging out of his coat and hanging it on a hook. The usual suspects sat at the bar and a small group occupied a table near the back, while a couple engaged in a game of pool. Walter dried a glass as he talked to Pete. Someone had selected "Grandma Got Run Over By a Reindeer" on the jukebox and decorations hung around the place, but otherwise, it wouldn't have been obvious it was Christmas Eve.

"Hey, Jackson!" Winston called. "You never did say what you're doing here on a night like tonight. Don't you have a nice lady friend you should be wining and dining?"

Pete stage elbowed him. "Don't you remember? He's got them problems..."

Winston looked shocked, then looked around. "And there aren't even any ladies around to help solve 'em."

They cackled in laughter as Chuck Thomas offered Jackson a sympathetic eye roll. "Lighten up, guys. It is Christmas Eve. And as far as I'm concerned, having Jackson back is the best gift this guy has got all year."

"I'd rather have that hot new waitress," Winston said.

Pete raised his mug. "Or at least another one of these."

None of the waitresses were working tonight, which meant if Jackson hadn't shown up to ask for his old job back, Chuck would have been on his own. Not that he couldn't have handled it…but he'd already asked if Jackson could hang out through closing so he could go home and at least surprise his wife at midnight with her gift. Jackson had readily agreed.

A short time later, Chuck left and he was on his own. Midnight came and went and as much as he hated himself for it, he kept checking his cell phone for messages.

Nothing.

Of course not. Why would she try to contact him after the way he'd treated her? Hell, he'd be lucky if she offered him a glass of water, even if he was dying of thirst.

Problem was, it wasn't water he wanted. It was her.

Damn.

The quickest way through any situation was straight. Gram had taught him andf Jason that when they'd been old enough to face mowing the massive front lawn. There was no sense complaining or bellyaching. It wasn't going to get done itself.

Only now, he wasn't sure which end of this mess was up, much less how to get through it.

His cell phone vibrated in his pocket. He was so anxious to answer it, he nearly dropped it in the sink.

"Hello?" he answered without looking at the display.

"Where the hell are you?"

His brother.

Shit.

He had no choice but to tell Jason he was working that night.

His brother didn't say a word. He merely hung up.

Great.

Jackson put the cell phone back in his pocket. Those at the back table were getting ready to leave. Good. Of course, the regulars at the bar wouldn't budge until he pushed them. But that was fine. He didn't have anything else to do anyway.

The front door opened. He glanced up from where he was pulling another draught for Pete to see his brother stalking inside. He put the beer on the bar a moment before Jason reached across the bar and grabbed the front of his shirt, dragging him across to the other side...

22

JACKSON STOOD STARING at his brother, expecting him to deck him after hauling him over the bar. Instead he merely stood staring at him, then his rough face broke out into a grin.

"Merry Christmas, little bro," he said, giving him a hug.

Jackson blinked, too surprised to do anything for a moment. Then he returned the unexpected affection.

"How are you doing?" Jason asked. "You look like you've lost weight."

"Careful, you're starting to sound like Gram."

Jason chuckled. "You going to get this old woman a beer?"

Jackson stepped around to the other side of the bar.

The regulars watched with interest but quickly

turned back to their own brews once the show was over.

Jackson popped the cap on an import and slid it over to his brother, then opened one for himself.

Often had been the time when the two of them would kick back and enjoy a beer, just shooting the breeze. But that was before Jackson had indicated a desire for involvement in Lazarus and Jason had thrown up a grease-covered wall he couldn't scale.

He squinted at Jason now. Obviously he didn't know what had gone down in Africa, or the life-saving hand Lincoln had extended. Otherwise, he wouldn't be so easygoing now.

Not that he'd expected him to find out. Lincoln was a man of his word: if he said he wouldn't tell Jason, he wouldn't.

Still, that didn't mean he wouldn't find out through other channels.

"Bet Gram had a fit when you left the house, considering it's Christmas Eve and all," Jackson said.

Jason grinned. "Nah...."

Jackson looked at his brother a little closer. Was it him, or did he appear to be... He searched for the accurate word.

"She and Jordan are enjoying some quality girl time together. I doubt they even know I'm gone."

Happy. That was the word.

Jackson grimaced and took a long pull from his own bottle.

Happy wasn't a word he usually associated with

Jason. Jokingly sarcastic, yeah. Driven, definitely. But happy…?

Of course, it wasn't long ago that love and his brother didn't mix, either. Then came an assignment that put Jason directly in Jordan Cosby's path, and his womanizing days were packed away in an old trunk. A very large old trunk.

Funny, Jackson thought, neither of them had considered themselves relationship material. They were both more career focused, the thought of being tied down enough to give them hives.

But now Jason was still grinning in a goofy way that made him look different.

"Okay, what gives?" Jackson asked.

"Huh? What?" He spun his bottle around, but didn't drink from it.

"I know it can't be sex. Gram wouldn't allow it unless you two were married."

"Oh, yeah? Try again."

Jackson raised a brow.

"Yeah, funny thing, that. Her only request? We not get anything on the rug."

They both chuckled loudly.

Jackson checked to make sure the remaining patrons were taken care of, then rounded the bar to sit next to his brother.

"So what's up then? While Gram might not have a problem with premarital sex—something I don't even want to think about at any time, but especially not tonight—what's the cause for the silly grin?"

It got even bigger, if that were possible.

"Well, you're not going to believe this..."

"After what's happened this past week? It's a pretty good bet I'll believe anything."

Jason looked at him. "You're going to be an uncle."

Jackson sat back. Jason looked as stunned as he was by the news, although Jackson was guessing his brother had had more time to digest the information.

"That's right. Jordan's pregnant."

"Wow!"

The usual asinine questions bolted through his head: How? Why? When? But he didn't ask any of them. Partly because he was too shocked to do much more than stare. But mostly because the shift of the floor under him made him take a fresh look at his own life.

"I know, right?" Jason said, finally taking a slug of beer. "You could have shot me point blank in the chest and I wouldn't have been more floored." He shook his head.

"What did you say? You know, when she told you?"

"Say? Not much. All I could do was grin."

Given the loss of their own parents at such a young age, both of them had always said they'd never get tied down, never have kids. Yet here was his big brother, about to be a father.

Wow.

He was having a hard time wrapping his head around the idea.

And an even harder time getting a grip on what it meant to his own longstanding beliefs....

"Gram's over the moon," Jason said. "She and Jordan have been talking nonstop about baby showers and weddings and nurseries ever since we arrived earlier."

Jackson drank nearly his whole beer in one draw, staring at the mirrored wall behind the bar lined with liquor bottles as if he'd never seen it before.

"Okay, what's up?" his brother asked.

Jackson looked at him. Images from the past week played like a slideshow against the blank screen of his mind. His role as Santa, Max sitting on his lap, Max sighing under his touch, Max's beautiful face earlier that day....

But it was Africa and Lincoln Williams that caught and held.

"I've got something to tell you," he said.

And he knew then that he had to confess all and face the consequences. He'd already decided to give up his bid to join Lazarus, following the career path his brother had wanted for him all along. And while he hated doing it on a night like tonight, and on the heels of learning such life-altering news, like with everything else in his life, the moment he decided to do it, there was no turning back....

23

New Year's Eve

HAD IT ALREADY BEEN a week since Christmas? Max found it impossible to believe. It seemed like just yesterday when she'd left Jackson's apartment, her stomach feeling leaden, her heart sitting in the middle of it.

"Come on, Maxi! Time to get our party on!"

She stared at where her Aunt Theresa had gotten out of the car, throwing her best wrap over her shoulders like she was a long-forgotten movie star putting on airs for the paparazzi.

Her mother had already gotten out of the driver's side and was smiling at no one and everyone.

Trying to figure out why she had ever agreed to come out with them—oh, yeah, the thought of sitting at home one more night sighing into her coffee cup had appealed to her not at all—she let herself out of the car. She didn't realize how close they were to The Barracks and Jackson's place until she looked down the block.

"What are we doing here?" she whispered.

"Bar hopping," her aunt said, taking one arm.

"We want to see which place is jumping the highest," her mom added, taking her other arm.

"Oh, no...." She dug in her heels.

Both women ignored her and pulled.

Suddenly she felt underdressed. It was a sensation she'd maybe felt all of five times in her life.

And all of them had been connected to Jackson in some way.

"You look fine," her mother said. "Stop fussing."

She hadn't realized she was until her mother had said something.

Yes, indeed, she was pulling at her white blouse and the brown distressed leather coat she had on over jeans and matching brown boots.

"You're young and you're freshly showered," her aunt said. "That's all you need."

Max couldn't help laughing at that.

"What?" Theresa said. "You really think any guy cares about the rest."

"Yes, well, good thing I don't really care about what any guy thinks, then, huh?"

Her aunt shared a look with her mother.

"Oh, shut up," Max said under her breath.

She wasn't sure how they knew, or how much

they knew, but it was clear they knew all too well the person she'd been "drenching her britches for"—as her aunt put it—was none other than Jackson.

She hadn't heard from him since before Christmas. And she hadn't expected to. Of course, that hadn't stopped her from checking her cell phone nonstop, just in case the impossible happened.

At any rate, he wasn't working at The Barracks anymore, so she didn't have to worry about running into him.

"What do you say we hit The Barracks first!" her aunt said.

"Let's go for it," her mother agreed.

An alarm bell went off in the back of Max's head. But by the time it stopped ringing long enough for her to think clearly, they were inside the bar. And she was face to face with Jackson.

She squinted. What was he doing wearing a Santa suit?

JACKSON'S RIB CAGE FELT suddenly too small. Just seeing Max again, well, if he needed a reminder of how powerful his feelings for her were, that was it.

Merely being in the same room sent his body temperature ricocheting off the charts, as if the sun had just broken a hole through the ceiling, flooding the place with golden warmth.

Of course, part of the reason for his high body temperature might be due to the stupid Santa suit he was wearing.

When Max's mother Cindy had called earlier in the day to say she was bringing Max by tonight, well, he had an idea....

One he thought might be so corny she'd laugh at him.

But it was too late now.

Well, except for the jacket.

He shrugged out of it and hung it on a bottle on the shelf behind him.

Now all he had to do was....

What?

His mind went blank.

The conversation with his brother in this very same place hadn't gone anything like he'd expected it to. Outside his surprise that he was going to be an uncle in six months, he would never have expected Jason's reaction to his Africa story, Linc's involvement included.

Once concluded, he'd braced himself for a torrent. Instead, Jason had remained silent for the longest time...then said, "And what are your plans now?"

That was it. No full front assault. No sucker punch to the gut for having gotten into trouble. No "I told you so" or "What in the hell were you thinking?" Not even a single "You're going to pay me back every dollar lost on getting your loser ass out of the jungle."

Just that simple question.

So he'd told him. "I'll concede you were right all

along. I'm not meant for Lazarus…or any other security detail for that matter."

His brother had looked around. "So this is going to be it, then?"

"Looks like. I haven't spoken to Chuck about any long-term plans, but I will. Maybe I can expand the kitchen, buy the old hardware store next door and turn it into a restaurant."

There was nothing wrong with those plans. He'd always enjoyed himself in the kitchen.

He'd just never thought he'd be doing it for the rest of his life.

Then Jason had said something that surprised him even more. "Find a girl, settle down, have a few kids…."

It was on the tip of Jackson's tongue to say he'd already fucked that up but good.

He'd squinted at his brother. "Yeah, just what you always wanted for me."

"No, it's what I wanted you to want."

"Difference being?"

"That you were never interested in it."

They shared a smile.

"Yes, well, I guess I'm interested now," Jackson offered.

Jason had looked at him closely. "Are you?"

No.

"Didn't think so."

Jackson hadn't quite known how to respond. So he didn't.

For so long he'd wanted to be a part of Lazarus. To work with his brother. To prove what he was made of. But his experience with Pegasus and the mission in Africa had proven the kitchen was where he belonged.

Then Jason took something out of his back pocket. A rectangular bit of paper that looked like a business card, but was creased and worn, as if it had been in there awhile.

He looked at Jackson, smoothing whatever it was out. Then he placed it on the bar and slid it toward him.

"What's that?"

Jason didn't answer. Instead he seemed to smile a bit as he took a silent swig from his bottle.

Jackson leaned forward. It was a business card. For Lazarus. But the name...

He'd blinked. And blinked again, certain he was imagining things.

But, no. Spelled out in neat type was something he'd wanted for so long, yet now that he had it, he couldn't quite bring himself to believe it.

His name.

"I don't understand. I fucked up."

Jason shook his head. "No, little brother, you didn't. You proved you have exactly what it takes. You not only got yourself and your men out alive, you did whatever you needed to, including calling Linc, in order to do it."

He still wasn't following him.

"The mission failed."

"Missions often do. You know that."

He did.

"What you did was realize you need others. That no mission is a solo mission. So welcome to Lazarus."

Now, a week later, the worn card was still in his back pocket. He was working everything out, letting it settle in. Jason had told him when he was ready, an office was waiting for him, along with a box of cards exactly like the one he'd given him.

That his brother had it planned all this time, was just waiting for him to learn…what, exactly? Blew his mind.

Speaking of things that blew his mind….

It seemed like an eternity had passed since Max had entered the bar along with her mother and aunt, yet it was only a few moments.

What had she told him the last time he saw her? That he wasn't alone?

At the time, he couldn't have felt any more so. Now?

Now he understood that it wasn't success that defined him—not only professionally but personally—it was the people he relied on, the people who relied on him.

The people he loved.

He made a move toward Max and she immediately tried to break ranks and run back out the door.

Jackson nearly vaulted over the bar, gaining the attention of everyone inside and earning a couple of wolf whistles. But Max was faster, rushing out into the parking lot.

"You better not hurt her any more than you already have," he heard her mother say as he passed.

He burst out onto the sidewalk, but she was still running.

"Max!"

She didn't break her stride.

Damn.

Clad in nothing but a T-shirt, his Santa pants, boots and suspenders, he gave chase.

A small voice in the back of his head told him this was dumb. She would have to stop eventually. He could catch up with her later, when she was open to the idea of talking to him.

But a louder voice told him he needed to catch her now and tell her what he'd been burning to tell her for years.

That he needed her forgiveness.

He caught up with her and caught her around the waist in front of a small, corner park. They both went down, falling into a snow pile.

She wriggled. He held fast.

"Shh," he whispered into her ear from behind,

unsure of why he was doing so. He just wanted her to stop fighting him. To look at him the way she had before.

After a few moments, she went still. But he didn't fool himself into thinking it was because she didn't want to be free.

The snow was cold against his bare arms and was beginning to melt through his T-shirt and pants. Still, he held fast, his restraining hold becoming more of an embrace as he worked her closer to him.

"Let me go," she whispered.

Jackson closed his eyes and rubbed his nose in her sweet-smelling hair. "I can't…"

She elbowed him sharply in the ribs, twisted his arm from around her and freed herself. She crawled quickly away on all fours. He caught her right foot and pulled her back down.

She had a couple more escape attempts—and a couple more falls—before they finally sat in the snow facing each other, out of breath….

She picked up a snowball and threw it at him, hard. It hit against the side of his face and slid down.

"Okay, I deserved that."

She threw another one.

"That, too."

She formed another one.

"The next you get back."

She hit him squarely in the chest.

"Okay, that does it."

He dived for her. She squeaked, her laughter like a salve to his battered heart as he grabbed a handful of snow and worked it down the front of her shirt.

She gasped. "No fair!"

"I warned you..."

They wrestled around.

"Get a room," a passerby grumbled.

He and Max watched him walk away in the other direction, then they burst out laughing.

He squeezed her hard against him. "You ready to call a truce?"

There was a moment's silence, then, "No."

"Okay, then marry me, and we can fight this out for the rest of our lives."

Jackson wasn't sure where the words had come from. All he knew was that after saying them, he'd never felt better about anything in his life.

She moved to elbow him but this time he was prepared. "No fair," she whispered so quietly he nearly didn't hear her.

He turned her so he could see her eyes.

"I'm sorry, Max."

She refused to look at him.

"I'm sorry for hurting you. I'm sorry for denying what I felt for you. I'm sorry for turning you away when I should have let you in."

She slowly met his gaze, her eyes bright.

He caressed the side of her face. "But mostly I'm sorry for not telling you this the first day we met."

He kissed her softly, lingeringly.

"I love you."

She made a sound between a whimper and a moan as he deepened his kiss. She melded into him and he held her tightly, letting her know he never wanted to let go.

And hopefully the response she was giving him meant he would never have to....

"Well, it's about damn time you two got it right."

Jackson reluctantly pulled back. They turned to find Max's mom and aunt standing on the sidewalk next to them.

"Now get up out of that snow before you both catch pneumonia and die before we get to enjoy the wedding we've been planning since you both were eight," her mom added.

"Seven," her aunt corrected.

"Whatever. Now, come on. We've got a new year to celebrate…"

Epilogue

A WEEK LATER, Jackson stood at the front of the Lazarus meeting room addressing ten of the best team members he'd had the honor to lead; first and foremost, Max, who stood near the front, her very essence seeming to light the room.

Whenever he wasn't at Lazarus planning this mission, he and Max were in his bedroom making up for lost time. A lot of it.

And he soon found himself wearing that silly grin that seemed to permanently widen his brother's face.

He was going to be an uncle. And a husband. And, soon, maybe a father...?

The idea nearly derailed his thoughts.

Nearly.

Included in the group were the five members from the failed Pegasus mission, none of whom had hesitated when he'd not only called them to come work for him, but to return to Africa. He felt pride in seeing them all standing there in front of him, alert and ready. Including Taylor.

"Okay, you're holding the mission plan in front of you," he said, referring to the thirty-page document he'd handed out as each member came in the door. "We leave in forty-eight hours. We'll be meeting three times before that to hammer out any further details. Questions?"

No one.

Good.

"See you at 1700, then."

The team members filed out of the room, leaving him and Max alone. She came to stand next to him.

"We're really going to do this, aren't we?"

He searched her face for signs of anxiety. There were none.

He grinned. "Yes, we are."

His first order of business, upon officially signing up with Lazarus, was arranging to go in after the hostages they'd been forced to leave behind in Africa. While he didn't expect their recovery would make everything all right, he did hope that it would mean the loss of so many lives in the original effort hadn't been in vain.

He'd also taken great pleasure in slapping a cease and desist injunction against Pegasus. If they tried to involve themselves in a similar mission, he would roll over them like an M1 Abrams Main Battle Tank....

Max surprised him by kissing him.

"I love you," she whispered.

"I love you more," he said back.

There was movement from the doorway and a few choice curse words filled the room. "Criminy, will you two at least shut the door first?" Jason asked.

His grin belied his true feelings as he slammed the door, leaving them alone.

"Now, where were we…?" Jackson asked.

Max hummed and rubbed her nose against his. "Right here, I think…"

* * * * *

PASSION

For a spicier, decidedly hotter read—
this is your destination for romance!

COMING NEXT MONTH
AVAILABLE DECEMBER 27, 2011

#657 THE PHOENIX
Men Out of Uniform
Rhonda Nelson

#658 BORN READY
Uniformly Hot!
Lori Wilde

#659 STRAIGHT TO THE HEART
Forbidden Fantasies
Samantha Hunter

#660 SEX, LIES AND MIDNIGHT
Undercover Operatives
Tawny Weber

#661 BORROWING A BACHELOR
All the Groom's Men
Karen Kendall

#662 THE PLAYER'S CLUB: SCOTT
The Player's Club
Cathy Yardley

You can find more information on upcoming Harlequin® titles,
free excerpts and more at www.HarlequinInsideRomance.com.

HBCNM1211

REQUEST YOUR FREE BOOKS!
2 FREE NOVELS PLUS 2 FREE GIFTS!

Harlequin

Blaze™

red-hot reads!

YES! Please send me 2 FREE Harlequin® Blaze™ novels and my 2 FREE gifts (gifts are worth about $10). After receiving them, if I don't wish to receive any more books, I can return the shipping statement marked "cancel." If I don't cancel, I will receive 6 brand-new novels every month and be billed just $4.49 per book in the U.S. or $4.96 per book in Canada. That's a saving of at least 14% off the cover price. It's quite a bargain. Shipping and handling is just 50¢ per book in the U.S. and 75¢ per book in Canada.* I understand that accepting the 2 free books and gifts places me under no obligation to buy anything. I can always return a shipment and cancel at any time. Even if I never buy another book, the two free books and gifts are mine to keep forever.

151/351 HDN FEQE

Name	(PLEASE PRINT)	
Address		Apt. #
City	State/Prov.	Zip/Postal Code

Signature (if under 18, a parent or guardian must sign)

Mail to the **Reader Service:**
IN U.S.A.: P.O. Box 1867, Buffalo, NY 14240-1867
IN CANADA: P.O. Box 609, Fort Erie, Ontario L2A 5X3

Not valid for current subscribers to Harlequin Blaze books.

Want to try two free books from another line?
Call 1-800-873-8635 or visit www.ReaderService.com.

* Terms and prices subject to change without notice. Prices do not include applicable taxes. Sales tax applicable in N.Y. Canadian residents will be charged applicable taxes. Offer not valid in Quebec. This offer is limited to one order per household. All orders subject to credit approval. Credit or debit balances in a customer's account(s) may be offset by any other outstanding balance owed by or to the customer. Please allow 4 to 6 weeks for delivery. Offer available while quantities last.

Your Privacy—The Reader Service is committed to protecting your privacy. Our Privacy Policy is available online at www.ReaderService.com or upon request from the Reader Service.

We make a portion of our mailing list available to reputable third parties that offer products we believe may interest you. If you prefer that we not exchange your name with third parties, or if you wish to clarify or modify your communication preferences, please visit us at www.ReaderService.com/consumerschoice or write to us at Reader Service Preference Service, P.O. Box 9062, Buffalo, NY 14269. Include your complete name and address.

Harlequin® *Desire*

ALWAYS POWERFUL, PASSIONATE AND PROVOCATIVE.

USA TODAY BESTSELLING AUTHOR

KATHIE DeNOSKY

BRINGS YOU ANOTHER STORY FROM

TEXAS CATTLEMAN'S CLUB: THE SHOWDOWN

Childhood rivals Brad Price and Abigail Langley have found themselves once again in competition, this time for President of the Texas Cattleman's Club. But when Brad's plans are interrupted when his baby niece is suddenly placed under his care, he finds himself asking Abigail for help. As Election Day draws near, will Brad still be going after the Presidency or Abigail's heart? Find out in:

IN BED WITH THE OPPOSITION

Available December wherever books are sold.

HD73139

Brittany Grayson survived a horrible ordeal at the hands of a serial killer known as The Professional... who's after her now?

Harlequin® Romantic Suspense presents a new installment in Carla Cassidy's reader-favorite miniseries,
LAWMEN OF BLACK ROCK.

Enjoy a sneak peek of
TOOL BELT DEFENDER.

Available January 2012
from Harlequin® Romantic Suspense.

"**B**rittany?" His voice was deep and pleasant and made her realize she'd been staring at him openmouthed through the screen door.

"Yes, I'm Brittany and you must be..." Her mind suddenly went blank.

"Alex. Alex Crawford, Chad's friend. You called him about a deck?"

As she unlocked the screen, she realized she wasn't quite ready yet to allow a stranger inside, especially a male stranger.

"Yes, I did. It's nice to meet you, Alex. Let's walk around back and I'll show you what I have in mind," she said. She frowned as she realized there was no car in her driveway. "Did you walk here?" she asked.

His eyes were a warm blue that stood out against his tanned face and was complemented by his slightly shaggy dark hair. "I live three doors up." He pointed up the street to the Walker home that had been on the market for a while.

"How long have you lived there?"

"I moved in about six weeks ago," he replied as they

walked around the side of the house.

That explained why she didn't know the Walkers had moved out and Mr. Hard Body had moved in. Six weeks ago she'd still been living at her brother Benjamin's house trying to heal from the trauma she'd lived through.

As they reached the backyard she motioned toward the broken brick patio just outside the back door. "What I'd like is a wooden deck big enough to hold a barbecue pit and an umbrella table and, of course, lots of people."

He nodded and pulled a tape measure from his tool belt. "An outdoor entertainment area," he said.

"Exactly," she replied and watched as he began to walk the site. The last thing Brittany had wanted to think about over the past eight months of her life was men. But looking at Alex Crawford definitely gave her a slight flutter of pure feminine pleasure.

*Will Brittany be able to heal in the arms of Alex,
her hotter-than-sin handyman...or will a second
psychopath silence her forever? Find out in*
TOOL BELT DEFENDER
*Available January 2012
from Harlequin® Romantic Suspense
wherever books are sold.*